THE NEW-CLASSIC S

SERI

of

SHORT STORIES FROM THE LIGHTER SIDE

BOOK THREE

Terminal Space

TREVOR WATTS

Dedicated to Chris Watts
For her editing skills, commitment and tolerance.

Log on to https://www.sci-fi-author.com/
Facebook at Creative Imagination

First Printing: 2020
Brinsley Publishing Services

BPS

ISBN: 9798600110540

CONTENTS

A HIGHER LEVEL

Gazing round this strange new environment, Lixia bristled her mandibles, and made the call. 'Lixia to Mothership. Come in.'

She waited only a moment, before, with a little trepidation, she called again. 'Lixia to Mothership.'

'Come in, Lixi. What's been the problem? You're two days late reporting back.' Captain Troid's voice was soothingly familiar, perhaps worried for her, but so welcome to hear.

'Sorry, Captain, I became deeply involved in the initial survey—'

'Right.' He cut her off. 'You're back on now. So what's the situation down there on the ground?'

She looked about her again. 'It's certainly a very different planet from Scalia, but, with a number of provisos, I believe we could survive and thrive here.'

'Oh? Elucidate.'

'Temperature range, air and general resources are well within acceptable parameters. In fact, it's a rather beautiful planet in its own way. It should certainly be habitable. In fact, I think I could find it quite lovable, really.'

'Okay, Lixi.' The captain cooled her down with his tone. 'Let's have the report, hmm? Have you detected any higher life forms?'

'Oh, yes, straight away, although they're not like us.' She hesitated, and straightened a few scales, and quick-licked them down to bring up the gloss. 'They don't have horns like ours, for instance. Although some creatures here do have horns of many sizes and shapes, they've not responded to any of my approaches.

'Even the beings with scales seem, I'm ashamed to say, almost blank-brained. They're almost entirely environment-reactive creatures, not truly sentient. It saddens me to say so, but even those with horns *and* scales—'

'Yes? The beings most like us?'

'Even they are scarcely aware of their own existence, much less being able to relate to others, or to a higher world.' There, that summed up the most closely-related beings on the planet – a disheartening situation.

'That *is* disappointing.' Captain Troid's voice took on a lower pitch. 'So we won't have any of our own kind to associate with?'

'Not really, no. Not of a similar physical form, anyway. But then, this planet is a weird one – bursting with life forms everywhere of one kind or another.'

'Yes? You said you had located an elevated form of life?' Troid sounded hopeful of a more positive outcome.

'I have, yes.'

'On a par with our own mentality, philosophy and awareness of the higher plane?'

'Yes. Perhaps even a higher level than we ourselves.' In truth, Lixia was impressed by their superior nature, but didn't want to overawe Captain Troid before he brought the rest of the crew and colonists down. 'I think we can learn much from them.'

'You've made some initial contact with their representatives?'

'Indeed. Yes, I have.'

‘Were they welcoming? Come on, Lixia… What did this higher life form say?’

‘Miaow.’

A TIME TO BE CULLING

'Roeth's a pleasant planet – nobody knows who found it first, us or the Qudsei,' Governor Mk'Kenny once told me when we were semi-socialising in M'hourat, his country residence. It wasn't long after I'd become Lord Commissioner. 'Historically, the records show that we humans and the Quds landed on opposite sides of the planet at around the same time. Whichever lot came second didn't notice the others.'

'Or didn't bother about them?'

'I suspect so,' he said. 'Our colonial bunch were reputedly in deep bother and didn't have much choice about whether or not to land, much less where, or who or what might have been there already. Maybe the Qudsei were the same.'

'Or too arrogant to care about lesser beings such as us?' I had a dim view of the Qudsei even then.

'Whichever, the Qudsei were quite a bit more technologically advanced than the humans, and initially, more populous, too. And they rather took over. Not exactly invaded and conquered our continent – it was more like they sauntered in and assumed charge.'

I remember thinking the Governor looked a touch Got-to-toe-the-line when he was telling me, 'The dat-streams say it was a benevolent partnership, and still is. With the Quds doing most of the providing. They had the technology that saved them work and time – and we thrived. The human birth rate sure overtook theirs. All across the planet, it was a case of small human communities finding a Qudsei family had moved in close by, or right there among them, building a large home complex for themselves, some facilities for work and leisure, trading, transport. Yesss, little communities mixing together – we didn't stick in single-race communes or anything like that.'

'Sure,' I semi-agreed. 'The way it's worked out – evolved – is like a ruling family and their humans, serfs, whatever we are to them.'

***

That conversation came back to me in the Moot Hall at Dawnington when Juli'arana came to chat with me on the subject during one of my open-talk sessions, practically continuing the conversation I'd had with Governor Mk'Kenny those six years before. 'Sure,' she said. 'Only it's become more apparent that they aren't quite so beneficent these days: we're getting the feeling that we're regarded more like nuisances, or playthings, of late.'

'We're supposed to be partners. Junior ones, maybe.'

'We're their pets, Commissioner,' she said. 'And with our numbers increasing much faster than theirs, they barely tolerate us.' It was Highday, my one day each viikko for people to talk with me about absolutely anything. 'And I reck they're becoming wary of us. "Too many humans living off us… Sucking us dry," I heard a couple of their eldermen saying a few days ago.' She imitated their sucking-in breaths so well.

'That chimes a little with me,' I said. 'I've been noticing a different mindset myself, these last few viikki. Mmm, yes, I think you're right, Juli'arana. I can see aspects of that in my other villages. Nothing specific, but—'

'They're living on past times, Commissioner Koyar. Look at their achievements since the Beginning: they've trained us, and that's about it. They've come up with no substantial technological advancements in the past seven-score years. *We've* done all that of late – the new deep rad units, the electron engines, the atmospheric cleansing, cure for turipsis. They think we're living off them, but my view is that it's become the other way round.'

This rang little bells inside, stirring thoughts I didn't know I'd been having. 'You think this attitude is part of a broader trend, Juli? With some greater significance?'

'Has to be. I've been looking much wider than merely within this region, Commissioner. Planet-wide analysis indicates eleven occasions of a temporary withdrawal of Qudsei families from a community – they all slope off on a mass family holiday, or something. Then it's like there's an open season on killing humans while they're gone.'

Oh shuggs - that's chiming in my head. What in Haydeze are the Qudsei up to?

'Digging into all these happenings,' Juli'arana continued, 'I found that Qudsei armour-squads had gone in. Insto-gas and dust, it sounds like. It's as if they're culling the family's rabbiat warren; clearing the excess numbers of pets down to more historic levels.'

'Manageable levels, maybe? And they don't want to watch?'

'It seems not. Their roboids are fast and lethal – they've been seen, weaponed-up, heading along the routeways. Not many human bodies are found. People vanish, generally overnight. It's a fairly consistent eighty percent of a settlement that vanishes, or dies within a few days. Brings our numbers down to less than theirs in all the settlements affected so far.'

'Sounds like a deliberate policy to ensure we're less troublesome?' Easy conclusion to come to when you have the wider data, not just one or two confused anecdotes from isolated settlements a thousand milta apart. 'So… are you suggesting we do something about it, Juli? Confront them. Retaliate? How?'

'Not up to me, Commissioner, but…' she hesitated, 'we could spread this as TS news, humans-only. Next time there's any sign of a Qudsei groupage preparing to leave, take a vacation, far-home visit, whatever, we use perathoxene on the Quds. A single shot to any of them in the family will spread among them; they'll be incapacitated for a time, and—'

'—Not kill them. A single dose isn't enough to set up a fatal intensity of reaction.'

'True, but they'd not be able to leave. If they wanted to keep out their community while their killing goes on, they'd be unlucky. And while they're debilitated, they'd be very vulnerable to a second, fatal, dose. They'd realise that. And they'd know they've been rumbled.'

'I spy a tiny problem with that, Juli: what happens then? We hope they stop doing it? Let them get away with all-but-wiping-us-out in nearly a dozen human communities already?'

'If they learned the lesson, and stopped, it'd save an all-out war that I'm not sure we'd win. The whole planet would lose the vast majority of its population.'

She took a drink. 'I shudder to think of the consequences.'

'And if the warren-keepers don't learn the lesson the rabbiats want them to? Suppose they upped their game, escalated the incidents?'

She hesitated, 'Er… I…'

'We'd have warned them. Then the Qudsei would do something overwhelmingly drastic to pre-empt us doing anything else, such as turn their roboids loose on us, or thoroughly dust huge areas with veanon powder. All at once.'

Juli'arana looked pensive, biting her lip. 'Perhaps we shouldn't? We ought to hold off?'

'We can't ignore it, not now we know. They'd carry on, getting bolder, killing us off with impunity.' My mind did its thinking in a whirl. *This is huge. They're killing us, on the quiet. This needs to be admitted to ourselves. And take appropriate action. Must think... think...* 'Koh. Do we have large supplies of perathoxene?' I asked.

'There is enough to start, to warn them off.'

'No, we've been through that. We need to hold off using it; build up a cache.'

'But we have to make a point with them, deter them.'

'No. We don't. I'm not thinking of deterring them, Juli. It wouldn't work. How long to have enough perathoxene in every community? High doses.'

'Well, it takes an oktu to mature a batch. So five oktus; forty days, all told? What are you thinking of? Laying them all out? Shouldn't we warn them what we could do? Give them an ultimatum?'

'Forget about warnings! Rabbiats don't warn their warren-keepers they're feeling restive and are going to take over the farm. We need to hold off any overt action or warnings for five oktus.'

Juli'arana didn't like the sound of that. 'What? We sit around while they kill off another dozen communities?'

'Not sit around. We'll use the time to make enough perathoxene to have maximum-strength doses in every community before we do anything to let them suspect. And in the meantime, we warn every community to be prepared to move out fast if the Qudsei look like they're packing their stuff away.'

'That'd surprise them… make them suspicious.'

'I don't care how suspicious they'd get. They won't find anything out: we'll not tell people exactly why we're suggesting they do that – maybe hint that their roboids have been known to go rogue when they're left without their Qudsei masters. We'll be ready to turn the tables on them: We need to wipe them out, entirely. Give them full-strength doses. We will choose one specific time, planet-wide – perhaps Meridian noon – in five or six oktu. We will exterminate them all at the same moment.'

'You're saying, "we will" – as though it's definite. Not "we would", or "we could". I wasn't thinking on that scale or so extreme when I came to you, Commissioner Koyar.'

'Well, I wasn't thinking about it at all – not being aware this was happening. But, if this's their attitude, it's them or us. They've started a war on us without declaring it. This *will* happen; they've already begun it. We could keep a few as pets, perhaps… specimens. museum mementoes? They don't breed quickly enough to ever be a numerical threat.'

‘Their technology still has the edge on much of ours. They’d win if it came to open conflict.’

‘Barely. If at all in many fields recently. But that proves what I’m saying, Juli: we have to go for all-out retaliation, before they fully get into the swing of culling us. Or in a position to go for us en masse.’

‘And suppose it’s *our* community, Dawnington, that suddenly finds its Qudsei are waving goodbye? Are we going to protect ourselves? Or throw our fate to the roboids, the same as we’re suggesting for everyone else?’

‘The same as for all; we stay alert and remain ready to move out at the first sign of the local Qudsei preparing to evacuate.

We both sat back. I was envisaging the inevitable carnage to come.

Juli’arana must have been doing the same. ‘We’d better keep our fingers crossed, then, Commissioner?’

‘And amass the ammunition.’

DEAR MAAR'JUH'RIH

My wife – who is a sperry – and I didn't marry for love. Not in the conventional sense. And sex has never been on our up-front agenda, although I confess that we do experiment from time to time, with varying degrees of joy and repulsion. No, indeed. We were both very clear about it. And that is not a problem even now.

It was just that we really jelled together in so many ways. She has such wit – I love her sense of humour, and she knows so much about all the cultural and heritage things from so many places. I speak seven languages; have a basic vocabulary in two light-pattern communication-forms; and a smattering of aromatische, and we both enjoy playing with words and trying to figure any common roots like Proto-Inyo. It helps us to get along, because we don't share the same birth language. Not that she was born, exactly.

We both love art and history, and have such different backgrounds and experiences that we're each a permanent joy of discovery to the other.

About sex: like I said, we do experiment sometimes, but it's been mostly inquisitorial. In the sense of we want to see if some of the old interplanex art holos, solidos and vids could possibly be real, or are they photo-manip fakes? Some of them are really old – over a thousand years, and have been of immense cultural significance on several planets for many, many years. And of scientific interest, too. Traditionally, many of these inter-planetary sexualic positionings have been considered extremely implausible, downright impossible, and inventions purely for the weird at heart.

You will possibly be wondering as you read this, if my Li-un Tatillonne and I have been attempting to replicate a number of these postures. And in this you would be correct. We have been most enterprising in our efforts to *discover* – not to prove or disprove any particular theory or treatise – if any of the ten most disputed sexual positions with the Perithralitic species is in fact possible.

This was progressing most interestingly, and without any disruption to our general lives here in Orbit Sphere 4X. Until a few cycles ago, when she greeted me on my return home from my overnight shift as Flight Officer aboard the Orbit-Surface Vessel Stellar Mary – with the words – and I quote, "klij burrrr wiki biv-biv?". Which, in case you aren't fluent in High Sperithium, translates as "Do my mandibles look fat in this?"

The thing is, I don't know how to answer. Or, indeed, if I should answer. Would it irrevocably alter our relationship if I were to even attempt an answer? Our relationship is not based on this kind of specific personal interaction, and this impinges on a non-entered-into aspect of our relationship. Should I answer, and lie? Or be truthful?

To make the matter more complicated, I have no idea how fat the mandibular structures of a Sperithium female should be to be considered fat, normal or slender. Or even if she is fishing for a compliment, and wants me to say, "Yes, wow, they look incredibly, beautifully fat in that."?'

I realise this may seem trivial, but it is really important to both of us. We swore that there would be no emotive-species-specific vanities coming between us. Li-un is as baffled as I am why she would do this. And yet, she insists that I answer.

Yours, in hopes of an early response, Ĝemanta Viro, Orbit Sphere 4X.

P.S. Please escalate your usual response time, as in the past two days, she has also asked me – in translation – "Do my tentacles look a bit frayed this morning?"; and "Have I got red rims round my eyes?"

To the latter, I responded, "Remind me which bits are your eyes today." I mean, how should I know? You know how Sperrys are – interchangeable body-part functions, and variable-design organic structures – one of the reasons I'm so fond of her is her infinite variety – although I do have my favourite combinations, of course, even if I'm never completely sure which part of her is which on any particular day. Her idea of red isn't the same as mine, anyway. Additionally, she won't say if red is a good or bad colour for her eye-rims to be.

***

Dear Ĝemanta Viro

You don't make it entirely clear which species you are yourself, and I wonder if this is part of your problem? Do you lack self-identity?

Basically, if you are one of the exoskeletal species, then you have deep, but solvable, problems here. They can be resolved through profound and meaningful discussions, beginning with clearly defining everything about yourselves in total honesty. Ask her what answers she would ideally like to receive from you. You must trust her, and give those answers without considering whether or not they are true. They are non-literal, litmus questions. There is no specific answer to them, for they are classic "Lie to me to show you love me" questions.

Give whatever answer she tells you she needs to hear. And pray that it is not the tenth day of her ovulatory cycle.

Do you both still wish to be in a non-love, non-meaningful-sexual relationship? Because it sounds very much as if, unsurprisingly, you have strayed far from that. It is quite clear that she wishes to take your relationship to the next level.

Depending on your exact species, Li-un may be gravid – pregnant by you, not via the normal self-impregnating semi-clonal reproduction. This is a typical behaviour of Sperrys at level 4b of their pregnancy.

If, however, you are one of the internal skeletal species, such as humanoids or polypterids, you need to read all of the above in the negative, and dissolve the marriage asap. In this case, the Sperrys, at this stage of a relationship, are working up to the Feast of the Consumption, in which the non-Sperry-partner is to be ritually eaten.

I hope this helps, and I look forward to seeing you on the menu,

Maar'juh'rih Ghruughs
Soking, Wurrey

HE'S IN MY QUEUE

Voik! In my queue. That's *him!*

I know I look especially stupid when my mouth hangs open like that. I stared. *It is you. Definitely. Come back to Yiquit. Just like that. And you're standing patiently in the immigration queue. Laughing and smiling. With a woman by your side.*

I've suffered from shock a few times, but not like this. *You.* All memory of him, for my own sanity cast into a back black corner of my mind. Never to be thought of again – the taint of my life. I didn't even harbour thoughts of vengeance. Not once in five years had I dreamed I'd lay eyes on him again, so there'd been no point in eating myself up with self-destruction.

But now… seeing him. *This is different.*

I switched to a different cam angle, and saw two small children in pushies. Practically babies; followed by an auto-bag. Not full, and the pushies are spaceport ones. *So you're in transit, calling back here after five voiking years? My Ex. You deserting yiker. With your whore and brat-springs. Showing them the scene of the crime, eh?*

I never once imagined you would come back here. Not after what you did – Nothing. One morning, 123 days after our wedding; 98 after arriving on Yiquit, you weren't home. A day's frantic checking, and found you'd left Yiquit on a morning shuttle into orbit, and taken a pass-freighter to Elkior, out in the Elkin Sector. I knew nothing more. A day later, I'd been evicted from our home – you'd sold it to pay for your ticket and job contract.

So the girls and I were in the gutters of Hellington North. With nothing except our clothes.

I checked the documents of the next person in the queue with my usual care. Studying faces and metadata simultaneously; nodding, pushing the Welcome button and smiling. And I watched *him* in the queue. *You keep glancing round as though you half expect to see me the distance. I bet you don't imagine you're taking any kind of chance calling back through here, do you? You must imagine I've been dead five years, hmm? Starved, or jailed for thieving – they're hard on aliens breaking their laws here. Maybe you think we've been deported, me and the girls. Your daughters.*

Voiks! To think I married you. I didn't really feel the need to, but the Yiquis prefer long-contract workers to be committed and proper, even after four years together. As if a plaspap certificate was going to make us any more stable and proper – quite the reverse, it seems.

There on my screen. Him. Joking with another passenger behind him. *Still the over-handsome face, so confident. The woman with you, smart little creature. Your new wife? Am I divorced? Or discounted? She looks much like I used to. Must be your type, eh? Younger version. I loathe you all – finger-wriggling pallid offspring included.* So suddenly, my heart thumping in hatred.

'Sorry… yes…' dealing with the next in the queue, a group of fixed-term contract-immigrants, as we had been. Some in the queue are vacationers – Yiquit has a lot to occupy a Tenday break. Most of this influx today are in transit, though. Some holdup at the Orbit Station Eki is causing a transjam – some problem with a couple of passenger cruisers brushing against each other – they'd be a few days re-obtaining their vac-worthy certificates. *Hmm... yes, the companies are putting you up for three nights, and laying on activities to keep you happily occupied. You didn't buy the cheap option, huh? You've got money now, have you?*

'Yes, yes, Madamya. Okay – one moment – I just need to check your iris and f.p ID.' Dealing with my queue with one corner of my mind; watching him with the other corner. The Yiquis are really fussy about who they let in, even for a few days.

'Yes, sorry about this, Sir.' I put up with the general chunter, but if someone in my queue wants to create, I have them sided. Security – in the shape of my senior officer, Ghast – escorts them aside, and we allow them to cool off, for however long it takes. Nearly always the males – of the five common species we get through here, it's only the spidies whose females are aggressive. Sorry – *arachnocanths*, not spidies. Whichever, if the rest of the family group has been sitting unfed and unwatered in the transit for a few hours, they don't usually want to cross me anymore. They acquiesce. Or… well, my record is six days while some idiot cooled off in the side rooms. His family caught the out-flight without him.

Ex is half-way to me now. I see him on my screens – side and overhead cams. Still out of direct vision to me. A little impatient with the queueing now. *You've got so much to learn about waiting.* The times I spent in queues – to give myself and the girls up – to throw ourselves on the mercy of a state that didn't understand the concepts of pity, compassion or empathy. They're a practical lot, the Yiquis. It was surrender ourselves to the state, or starve, or be dropped in the desert as a vagrant.

And you didn't give yourself to the state for free – you had to earn your piecrust for an age, before you got to the meat inside. Like two days work – cleaning floors in the lounges, before they let us eat anything. Another six days before they let us into a dorm room with other deserteds and destitutes. A few human, but mostly shellies and spidies who weren't so keen to work. They preferred to lay and stupidly hope someone would rescue them. So, with the others being reluctant, there was plenty of menial work for me to do. The idlers were escorted out after their ten-day adjustment period, in the direction of the far wastelands. There must be some awfully big bone- and shell-yards out there.

Yimmy, Yaney, Yasminy and I worked. I had them picking up litter, emptying bins, wiping surfaces, tidying paps and packages – transit passengers can be such thoughtless creatures. To the extent that they were always leaving their belongings behind – IDs, comms, keyters, jewellery… even little kids sometimes. They mostly remembered pretty quickly, but not always, and I started up a lost and found desk – a broken one they let me repair and keep in a corner of the lounge. A few folk were grateful, and maybe gave me a tip in some weirdo currency.

Between the work sessions, tiny Yazz would hold a bin while I wheeled her round picking rubbish up

Set myself up with an account once I had some savings – about eight days' work credit that I could bank into a fingernail account, and I started charging a fee for findings – small – admin only. All profit. The Yiquis didn't want to know – we were keeping the whole transit lounge clean, smell-free and happy with returned properties – at such little cost – a pittance wage after a time, a bedspace in the jail-dorm, and a table I'd fixed.

Course, I accidentally killed a couple or so transies in the dorm. They crack open so easily, the spidries – three trying to rob me on separate occasions, and one utter perv who thought he was into antenna-ing my girls. Yoiking perv. They dumped him, antenna-less in the drylands beyond Aridity somewhere, with the rest of the rubbish. Probably eaten by the tigerats that scavenge round the dumps – quite aggressively, I understand. Hope it was slow and pain-wracked – pervy shugger. Nobody came out the desert; not ever.

Profit and work ethic are the foundations of Yiqui society and economy. You got to earn your place; then keep your place.

I learned fast and hard. With my tinies to look after, I did everything except sell myself along the concourse. Though, it burns me to recall, I sometimes spent time with passing high-up Yiquis. They were curious about human anatomy, habits, social mores, before they travelled into TerraFed systems. They wanted to be Oh Fay with such things, and expressed their satisfaction in a generous financial manner.

I buzzed. Had a word with Ghast – He's a tall guy with pincers to die for – and showed him the cam-shot of this suspicious-looking human down the queue. Printed it off so he could be sure – the Yiquis really do have difficulty telling us apart. So Ghast sidled off down the line, counting to number twenty-three and the yellow-striped travelcoat, while I dealt with the next one. 'Straightforward transit person, stranded for a three-nighter – no problem, Ma'am. Have an enjoyable time on Yiquit – yes, we do try to be extra-friendly here…'

Ghast was back. Ex's wallet, ID, smarf, keyter, all in a little plaz-pack sliding onto my desk. 'The male is in Security Room Three.'

'Thank you, Ghast. Perfect. He's the one. We humans look so much alike, don't we?' I flicked a few pics of Ex and other passengers across the screen.

'Indeed,' he agreed. 'You are all so similar.' He'd never be able to tell Ex from any other human without a full biometric-pic in the future. *So now Ex is sided off, without ID or cash. Now, who'd been in that position five years ago? Such a warm thought now.* 'Hmm. I wonder, Ghast, if we should do a little extra check? Hmm? Perhaps you might ask the next five males in line to step into Security Three as well – okay – females, males, whatever. It's not obvious with the avvies, is it? Five of anything – put them in there with him. Yes, let them keep their ID, don't want *them* getting lost do we? Just while we carry out a little check.'

It was maybe a dozen minutes before Ex's whore and her brood of two were next up. I took my time with the couple before them, using the time to eye up my replacement, fretting beautifully behind them. Looking all round for her erstwhile companion. *Yes, you vitch – you have a lot of fretting to do… An awful lot of fretting.*

‘Ghast? Would you like to let the Security Three detainees out now, hmm? Only the ones with ID. Undocumenteds must remain in there.’ Ghast wouldn’t know one from another, so Ex would stay and Ghast wouldn’t recall that he was the first one in there. *Mmm, how angry... frustrated, you’ll be. Won’t help you at all. Security knows how to deal with malcontents and complainers like you. Nothing to do with me now: I’ve passed you over to them. Byeee. Ex. You been exxed.*

Now then, ‘Next. Mrs? Ah… name? Mirinya? Oh yes, travelling alone? No? With your two children, I see? Lovely little lookers.’ *Spit-roasted, they’ll make a nice table centre-piece at a Yiqui banquet.* ‘Your travel documents? No? ID? No? Your hubby has them? Where’s he? Oh dear… We have no record of… I’ll check.’ *You skyla – you could be my sister – much younger sister. Know how to look after starveling babes, do you? With not a cred or a friend or a roof over your head? How delicious, what you’ve got coming and you have no idea, have you? Any more than I had.*

‘Let’s see – you have your own ID? Means of support? Ticket to leave? Somewhere to stay? No? Oh dear… It’s all with whom?’ I glanced down at the plaz pack, ‘Oh dear, there’s no record of such a person; not in the ship manifests or landing numbers.

‘Erm, let’s have a look… No… I’ll check through immigration… No no; sorry, I don’t see…’ *Stupid glott, you’re believing it all. Such naivety. The young, huh?*

‘Perhaps you’d like to wait in one of our side rooms for a short while?’ *Maybe ten days in the destitute dump room? Hmm? You pert-faced little skib.* ‘I expect this'll be sorted out, before the queue is transited through – won't take long – yes, so sorry for the inconvenience. Oh, yes, I know – it can be so upsetting, can't it?' *It'll get much much worse – find out what the pre-dorm dump is like before you go and explore the desert, hmm?*

'I'll come to you myself when I'm done here, if it hasn't been sorted by then. Yes, of course all will be well.' *I'll have his balls for earrings by then. And I'll gloat over them whenever I wear them.* 'Yes… there's a cosy little dorm lounge where you can make yourselves comfortable. I don't expect it'll be long.'

Ghast is talking with him in Sec Three, where I can listen in on my set. *Complaining like that won't help: Ghast won't understand. It'll just raise his pincers and shell hairs. So now you're threatening, you and all your powerful connections. No help at all.*

'You're the only one here,' Ghast was repeating to him. 'The others have gone. They had ID, means of support and departure. You have nothing. We'd better check your record here – coming in clandestinely, are you? Vagrant? Criminal? Have previous here, do you? Wanting to avoid officialdom?' Ghast could be wonderfully obdurate and non-comprehending. It's just how the Yiquis are.

Ex was one day in Sec 3; with no food – he hadn't earned it. Then he was causing more trouble, refusing to answer, shouting, violent towards Ghast…

'The vagrant immigrant had to be sedated,' Ghast reported. 'It appears that while he was unconscious, he underwent a small operation before he was taken to a desert site for further detention. And then to Cactus Camp when his attitude and cooperation didn't immediately improve.' *Ah, ex-hubby dear, you'll have to work very hard to earn your way out of there – no-one has done it yet. Ever. A skeleton already, are you? Picked clean in hours, they always say. Keeping company with the mocho lizards, hmm? Best place for you.*

Oh Ghast, you're so good. It's why I chose and appointed you myself. Several years of experience working with the Yiquis, dealing with them, accommodating them, learning to live among them. They accept me as the best alien thing since diced oysterbread fritters. I'm clean, efficient, bright and I keep the visitors in line, non-complaining and positively happy. Visitors never commit even the most minor of crimes on my watch, and I'm paid out of Immigration Department funds, Customs, Security and the Visitor Bureau. They simply haven't realised they're all paying me separately. Or choose not to realise.

I've done quite nicely in the past year or two – after the utter direness of the first three here. Well paid and high position now; villa; responsibility for immigration and transit; and for human welfare and liaison. *How're you coping, eh, vitch? Five days now. If you're still in one piece – sorry, three pieces – you'll all be out on the desert dump before the end of the Tenday. Join what's left of him.*

That was a Pit of a night. Pits! I tossed and thrashed, and had the visions as never before…

You'd antenna my girls! I'll rip your… Nothing to eat… Precious… Yasminy… hush your crying. Yimmy, I'm sorry… Faces looming and snarling so close… We need to… Voiking Gods! I hurt too… too much… mustn't show it… Vile spidry… We shall survive… My children will… Shuggit, the pain… starving… Must work… must survive… Whatever I have to do… Be strong… be strong… do anything… anything… Nobody robs me of what I slaved for… claws snapping and snipping at us… I'll rip you apart and feed your globin to the rats… I shall survive… My children will live – regardless. No crying…. Never cry… It's weak…

Drowning in sweat. Exhausted by the thrashing, the ghastly torment of the night… Voik, I was so strong back then. So strong. Nobody else would have survived, not with their children. So strong… I had to be.

How's she? And hers? I bet she's not as strong as I was. She'll be suffering. Good. And her brats? Her maggots?

I logged in. Seeing inside the dump lounge. She was alive; barely coping. Very weepy. Trying to protect her offspring. Not determined enough to survive with her kids. Not skilled enough. Very weakened, run down. Not enough inner strength.

Come on, vitch – if I could do it…

Yeah, if I could do it…

But you can't, can you, vitch? You're not capable. You're going to die, aren't you?

Voikit! You can't do it can you? You don't have my strength. What you done wrong? Anything you knew of? Ever heard a word about me? And his first three children? I bet not. Not a hint. You didn't know, did you? Nor did I.

I cut the screen.

You could be my sister, you vitch. My own kids looked so much like that. Such innocence at that time of life. I always fought for myself and mine…

Yikes! Is this the time to do something positive – not selfish – in my life? Like rescue a suddenly-stranded family?

No voiking chance. Whoever helped me?

That Yiqui cleaner who was leaving. She helped me. Told me about having to earn your way out the dump dorm. Said about her job… if I took it over…

And what's this vitch doing, apart from sobbing and clutching all night with the brats? Yeah… working in the caff-bar… not earning enough to ever get her out of there… pathetic…

Should I see her? No. Never. *You promised you'd call in – six days ago.*

Pushing the key-tap away, I called to Ghast that I would be taking ten, and I went to seek her out.

Hollow-eyed. Big-eyed kids. Voik! Mine were identical at that age. These could be mine.

'Him? I understand he was released,' I told her, 'just before the transit connection. I was led to believe he left, with a companion. I assumed it was you, and that all was settled. I'll look into it. Meantime, perhaps I could find somewhere a little less gruesome for you and the little ones?'

Why the voik did I say that? I've no intention of... 'Look, come with me. At my home, I have a side suite for visitors and on-site workstaff. You'd be more comfortable, and certainly the children would. Not far from here. You could walk in to work. I employ a Yiqui girl to help around the house and garden. She'd love more to do, like training up to look after the littlies. No, no charge; I don't expect my guests to pay.'

'Mirinya? His creds, cards and documents have been found on the Queen of the Starways. Yes... seventy days since he left here. After a stop on Mairn. He must have forgotten them, lost them; or he may have dumped them as a deliberate mislead. He could be anywhere, or nowhere. I'm sorry. Everything will be returned to you, whatever he had.'

'You're still working in the caff-bar in Transit? There's a scuff'n'coffista opening round the corner from here on Vikos Avenue. They're advertising for staff, including a manager. I believe they're wanting to attract the human passing trade on their way to and from the terminus. You could be the ideal candidate.'

We may be true friends someday, Mirinya and I. Our children are so well suited together. You'll never know about Ex. Or me. And you'll never even suspect what my unusual earrings really are.

I DON'T CARE

'No. I'm not going to help. I don't care tuppunction what you or anyone else says or does.'

I scarcely heard their pleas, my neighbours and colleagues around the community. 'No,' I confirmed. 'It's not going to happen.'

I stayed in the cabin of my heavy wagon, and patiently waited until they'd finished. 'I don't care – I won't take my rig across there to help them. *I. Don't. Care.'*

'Come on…' They tried to persuade me. 'We're all friends now. We're at peace with them.'

But I was adamant. 'I'm not at anything with them or anyone else. Not peace. Not war. Never was.' I shrugged.

'They're trapped, stranded. Their craft's stuck. They need you. You *must* help them.'

'No, I mustn't. They're nothing to me. Never will be. I don't do helping.'

'Have you no humanity? They'll die.'

I shrugged again. 'Nothing to do with me.'

'It's because it's them, isn't it? The Monitees?'

Totally uninterested, I checked the lever settings on my Max-4 Lifter. Automatically, I wiped a speck of dust from the dashboard.

'Prejudiced, are you?'

'Speciesist?'

'The wars are over.'

'What they ever done to you?'

'Done to me?' I looked blankly round, 'Nothing that matters. Not any longer.'

'So why? They only need helping out of there. You have the equipment. It'd cost you next to nothing to help them.'

'No.' I tapped the startup code in.

They badgered on – calling me all sorts, as though insults would persuade me. They resorted to threatening me, describing the terrible consequences for the Mons if they didn't get help – the awful death that awaited them. 'How would you feel?'

'I'd feel exactly the same as I do now – utterly indifferent. They can rot, asphyxiate, starve, whatever they want. Makes no difference to me.' I started the motor. 'It's my home time.'

Out the side window, I could see the damaged Monitee craft. It had stumbled, toppled onto its side. To say it had crashed would imply being wrecked and destroyed, and it wasn't that bad. But it's not going to move again, not without help. From me. *But why should I care?*

'Yeah, I see them. They're not going anywhere. That's alright. I don't care.' I tried to think myself into the Monitees' place, 'Maybe they enjoy sitting there. Or whatever they're doing – standing, kneeling. Nothing to do with me.'

'You're dead inside,' one of them shouted.

That's no way to endear yourself to me, I thought.

I don't get arm-twisted by bureaucrats, do-gooders and professional band-wagoners into anything nowadays. I haven't let that happen since that year I spent with the Monitees.

Sure I got the equipment. It's not a huge job. Cost me nothing except a couple of feds' worth of power. But they didn't want to hire me to do a job: they wanted me to do it, 'just out the goodness of your heart.'

Doing a heart-powered freebie comes way behind going home to relax with the felini. I don't do freebies unless it's something or someone I care about.

The list of things and people I care about hasn't even reached one yet – I was gonna put my own name at the top. But I didn't bother.

Let them sit, smile, writhe or rot. I don't care what the Monitees do.

If this lot want to carry on ranting at me, appealing to my better nature, they'll discover I don't have a better nature than the one on parade right now. Then I'll leave to get away from it, and they'll find themselves without the only heavy odd-jobber in the community. That'd see them in the skrawks in no time, the rate they get mired down, collapsed on, stalled, seized up and run into. I'll take my heavy equipment and move away. They can join their Mony friends on the dead heap. I don't care.

The Monitees, yes. I remember sometimes. Not that I care. I keep an ID card round my neck, mostly to remind myself who and what I am. I used to show it to people who thought I was weird. Now, I don't bother. I don't care what anyone thinks. They can think what they want. I think what I want. Why would I bother explaining to anyone?

Back then a few years, I was one of a dozen-strong prospecting team. We were looking for minerals on a promising moon called Nulaar. And one blazing day, a hundred fully-armed Monitees dropped on us. It was right back in the earliest days, when there hadn't been any sign of trouble between us. I'd sure never even seen any before – scarcely knew what they looked like. But there they were, half as big again as me, with eight arms and an insectoid head. There was no way a gang of civvy mecho-workers was going to fight them off with drill bits and XRF analysers.

Looking at my ID card – yes, I do remember. I was held prisoner for a year. They returned us when the Federation-Monitee conflict was over. Our Fed doctors tried their best to get me back to how I was before. But there was nothing they could do. That was okay. I didn't care then. I don't care now.

The Monitees experimented on us, wanting to learn about humans, to comprehend us before they launched major attacks on any of our colonies or planets.

Emotions were beyond their understanding, and how they affect the working of the human brain. 'Sentiments… passions… feelings, are the essence of humanity,' one of them told me. 'They are unique to humans. We wish to study them, extract them. We want to understand how a human brain works without them.' And they started their operations and experiments on us.

The last operation they did on me was an empathy bypass.

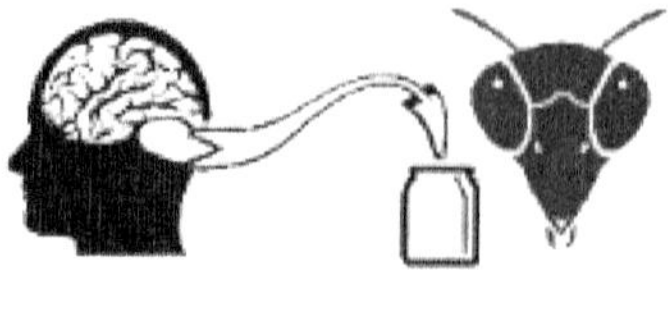

I'M A SQUUMAID

I'm just a normal girl, they say.
I'm pretty and bright, with a gorgeous pair
Of ankles and eyes and the rest in between.
To add to the charm, I'm also blonde.

Well, sort of blonde – my hair has an amber sheen,
And it's very attractive, some men say.
'More like a salmon shade,' said Ray,
My boyfriend then. 'So rare to see.'

He'd stroke and caress my flowing locks,
Until he noticed my scent one night.
'What's that?' he sniffed.
'Is it Eau de Cologne, from Germany?'
'No, it's from further afield than that,' I said.
'It's Eau de Squid, from the Philippines.'

So it was 'Goodbye, Ray,' and 'Hello, Joe.'
But Joe was a drinking man; he'd have a few
And get into rows with his mates
In the Fisherman's Grill
Then it was home to me in a narky mood,
His thoughts not on love, but on fighting still.

One time he decided to pick on me.
But my skin turns to shell, like a carapace,
At any threat.
To his disbelief, it broke his fist
And he howled in pain and sobbed in shock

Then across the room I reached as he tried to flee,
And gripped him with my toes.
'They're lobster claws!' were Joe's
Last words. 'On the end of your feet!'
He shrieked anew as I gripped so tight
And taught him he really shouldn't
Be quite so awfully cross with me.

So it was 'Cheerio, Joe,' and 'Howdy, Willy.'
My darling Willy adored the way
My body can coruscate with patterned lights
That flicker my length from toe to crown
Or gill to gut as we like to jest around the reef.

I'm quite a sight in a darkened room,
When I nakedly stand like a Christmas tree
With my body-lights on in full display;
All flashing in sequence according to mood
Or the music we play.

And when I swayed in such a way,
It drove my Willy wild
And he desperately sought
To increase the thrills
By wiring himself
To a disco set
With all the frills.

But he wasn't as good as he thought he was,
With the dance, or the lights, or electrical skills.
My poor dear Willy went *up* in smoke
And *down* like a frog with barely a croak.

My stomach tube has a mind of its own.
When I'm really starved,
It just pops out and reaches round.
Snaking round, seeking food,
It envelops its prey and sucks it in.

Such a surprise for New-Boy Nige
When we went for a meal at the Mexican Hat:
His prawn chimichanga I couldn't resist.
Unknown to me, my tum-tube slid
Under the table and over his knees.

Beside his plate I saw it rise,
And I had to squeal and wave
To distract him then
As my tentacle sniffed and swallowed the lot.

He wondered where his meal had gone,
So safely tucked away in me.
I suggested a pork burrito instead,
But there was still a touch of suspicion there.

When I burped again with a breath of prawn,
He said not a word, but he sniffed all night,
And was gone by dawn
And I never saw my Nigel again.

But Tony was there to help me out.
'Your eyes can widen, like saucers of milk,'
My Anthony said, 'so full of cream,'
And gazed in my depths of coral caves;
And saw my shipwrecks lying there.
He shuddered twice when he hit those rocks
And foundered deep.

'Full cream, that's you,' he murmured low,
'But my stomach's weak
And I only drink the semi-skimmed.'
But I could never go for that,
So I sucked him into my milken eyes,
And drowned him there
And flushed him out like cod liver oil.

Breathless once when playing with Clive,
I opened my gills and waved them round
For the extra air I needed then.
My secondary heart, of course, popped out as well
to flush itself and ding like a bell.

Clive was amazed but he took it well;
Considering the way they flapped and fluttered
In time with the band on the radio.
But I went off Clive when he confessed

At the Ocean Grill,
With a pesto made of basil and dill
That his favourite starter was a deep-fried plate
Of calamari rings with a peppered dip.
'Yeuk Yeuk – You cannibalistic pig,' I said,
And I showed him where he should stick

His battered rings.

'I'm an Oceanic Biologist,' my Larry gushed,
And says I'm a wonderful blend
Of pleasure and work.
'I adore the way you slide under the door
And slink into bed like a tentacled whore.'

I cuddle him there with suckers all over my arms
And tentacles so neat and trim.
It delights him then, when he guides my hand
In bed and finds I still have another five
To tickle his fancy and play with him.

My tentacle pair wrap twice round Larry
To keep him close,
I pulsate in time to encourage him more.
When the light comes on in early morn,
I'm back to me, his lovely girl,
All salmon blonde and a lovely pair.

There's so much more I can share with him
Like extrude my stomach out my mouth,
Fully inside out, and taste at him and his sexy bits.
He closes his eyes and likes to dream
I'm kissing him with shrimpy cream.

My best-ever trick, he says, was when
I splattered the walls in inky black
That squirted out the tapered spout
Of my extra hypo-branchial gland.
'A wonder you are!' he exclaimed in joy.
'My Melanin, my Little Miss Right.'

We said we'd bathe together tonight,
In the new hot-tub in his little back yard.
So secluded, and hung with trees like coral fronds.
'You'll feel at home in there, alright.'

Yes, yes, I'm really looking forward to it.
I can propel myself with jets so strong
I'll be round the tub in two seconds flat,
And spinning twice like an acrobat.

If we toss in the fish from the koi-carp pond
I'll show him how I catch and skin and fillet them
With just my teeth and my inborn knack,
And spit out the bones in a little sac.

But most of all, I'm wondering now,
When we're snuggling there and taking a nap
Is how he'll react when I squeeze down the drain,
And come out the tap.

LAKE N'KARA

The invitation was there on the board in the Student Union. It didn't give a lot of detail about exactly where the proposed expedition was heading for, but it would be for, "two months of sheer discomfort, isolation and ornithological research."

'Africa,' was the dark whisper among the undergrads, 'up the highest, hottest and most desolate mountain that Prof can find.'

'Looking for birds.'

As someone had just broken up very acrimoniously with his bird, and wanting to get as far away from the UK as I could for the summer, I knew it was for me. 'Especially,' I told the Prof when I dug him up in the Level 2 cellar, 'as I do geography and geology, so I know where Africa is.'

He huffed and chuffed and clearly didn't want a mere jack-of-all-subjects geographer, but he was moderately polite about turning me down, 'No. You're not what I'm looking for.' He wasn't what I was looking for, either – skinny, wispy-bearded little old swat who lived in the library and the biology exhibit stores. But I was prepared to put up with him, so why wouldn't he return the sentiment? He'd disappeared up a stuffed emu's back end by then.

'Never mind,' I said.

Not easily put off, I loitered round the notice board and listened to the gossip, innuendo and speculation. And decided I really had to go – it was almost certainly to a high mountain plateau in Aruna, East-Central Africa, with Lake N'kara at its centre. Prof had been researching it for a year, and was apparently convinced there was a new species of flamingo-like birds inhabiting the margins of the lake.

A couple of Mairaid's friends were in Zoology, and they said he was having trouble keeping the trip together, what with all the political and social unrest in Aruna, 'And Prof being such a wanker… Totally in his own world. Forgets everything unless it has feathers. Utterly clueless about relating to people.' So spending two months camping and twitching up a baking, gunfire-raked mountain didn't appeal much to anyone.

'I'm still in a with a chance, then,' I decided. 'Just my cup of arsenic.' Particularly after four male members suddenly dropped out in favour of a humming-bird survey in Costa Rica, with hotel accommodation. If only I could claim the credit for spiking his trip, but I gathered it was a rival lecturer who had – supposedly unexpectedly – received the offer of a substantial grant, with a short-life take-up date on it. Two of the girl students backed out, too, because the fellers weren't going any longer. Which left a trio of foreign girls and two young men who were a couple. Or so it was said.

Bulling up on birds of the central African highlands and lakes was easy enough – a week of late nights –

and I happened to bump into Prof on the stairs one evening when there were only the two of us staying late. So I happened to mention the trip and I was still available, and, 'Perhaps I should have told you about my hobby – I'm fascinated by wading birds of Africa…' and I waxed lyrical until he relented.

'Alright. You can drive? You're healthy? Any knowledge of that region?'

'Of course, if it's really Lake N'kara you're heading for, then I know the area quite well, there's a volcano not fifteen miles away, Ngoro goro. Constantly in a low level of eruption; it has a fire lake and everything. I went there last year.'

So that suckered him in, and I was in, too. Whichever direction we approach it from, I came from the opposite direction last year, so I'm not familiar with this precise route. If only I could have afforded to do that trip last year – I craved to climb Ngoro goro. It would have been a fabulous addition to my Ph.D. As it was, all I had to do now was wait for the judgement on my thesis. Then off to NZ for a job as junior vulcanologist in Auckland, other things being equal. Like these headaches not getting any more frequent.

Okay, so the unrest in Aruna was becoming more akin to a war, but, if two Dutch girls and a German could go, so could I. What's a bit of risk, eh? While I'm young, irresponsible and feel like I've got nothing to lose. Prof tried to make my acceptance provisional, hoping for more applicants, but that was a vain hope – all the copies of his notices round the Student Union were in my bin. So, in desperation, he pretended to re-interview me, but we both knew I was in, and I said maybe I might stay on afterwards, and have a couple of weeks on Ngoro goro by myself.

'Reckless bliss,' I told myself. 'And it's only two weeks away.

'I'm the best of a bad lot,' I told Prof. 'You haven't got any choice about me if you need a minimum crew of six.'

We had a series of meetings, the twosome and the trio, plus Prof plus me. Talk about unenthused. I had to wonder about why the other five were coming. The girls huddled together and spoke culturedly in what they thought was better English than Prof and I spoke, but was actually polished up from US Forces Radio, and sounded rather pseudo-silly. The two guys just huddled together, holding hands. I was beginning to look at Prof rather fondly. In comparison.

The rumours of unrest in Aruna intensified, along with coverage on Google. Prof and I plotted the supposed spread of active dissent on the maps, 'Come on, Prof, we know the info's mostly false and totally out-dated.'

'Of course, but the rebel forces have evidently stalled around fifty miles west of Lake N'kara. Reportedly setting up there for the wet season where they have a commanding position overlooking the Rift Valley.' The girls were apparently undeterred, but the two guys looked at each other, and the rest of us. And they muttered a lot.

'Perhaps you should have paid even closer attention to these news reports, Peters.' Prof gave me his Disdain Level Five look when we consulted the latest laptop news at Heathrow.

‘Sure, all my fault, is it?’

‘Of course, you reckless little turd. You’ll not worm your way in with me any more than you will with those three.’

Me little? I’m a foot taller than you are. Just because I crack a funny now and again, he thinks I’m not serious about anything. Huh. Bet he’d listened to what Mairaid’s friends were loudly saying about me, too. Personally, I never listened much to Mairaid, much less her Irish colleens. I learned more that way.

Armed military groups had been seen forty miles away at Kitshas; the government was increasing its armed presence in the region; local tribal leaders were unhappy about that – they were regarded as enemy tribes that the government forces were likely to take it out on, too. For old time’s sake. ‘But which reports do we believe, eh, Prof?’

The other thing I’d gleaned, and not told him about, was that Mount Ngoro’s roiling lava lake was increasingly restless, too, with the inner crater overflowing. So the great caldera of the outer crater was steadily filling up now – the satellite pics looked fabulous. I planned to clear off in that direction once the birdy twitchers were settled and happy. I desperately wanted to scale that most active of volcanoes, while I had the chance. I could hike there in a couple of days. But my conscience keeps poking, and telling me I’m bound to the prof and the expedition. And anyway, the rains had come early and torrentially, with unheard-of levels of flooding in the Rift Valley, causing a lot of unpredicted migration of wildlife.

‘But that’s mainly along the valley, not up into the highlands. Sorry, Prof.’

So we had lots to look forward to when we landed at the other end.

At the scrubby little regional airport, our stores, sent out two days earlier, had been raided – half the food was missing. So we needed to buy local replacements to take with us. The fuel for the two Land Rovers had been confiscated by someone official, but we could buy it back at some extortionate rate; along with the spares crate. I had a huge, really silly row with some massive guy with a sub-machine gun and a four hundred litre horde our petrol. Cost me a price rise and a broken nose. He was dead accurate with the satin metal butt of that PP41. I think I wet myself when he stuck the other end in my mouth. Dunno why.

Prof wasn't to be put off: his expedition had been ten months in the planning, since he'd investigated reports of unidentified birds populating the very high-altitude and isolated Lake N'kara, which was known mainly for remaining water-filled through the dry season. 'Fed by underground springs,' he decided over the top of his rimless glasses. 'Largely fresh water, not alkaline.'

Matters eventually picked up at the airport, and, despite the heat and dust and flies, things didn't become any worse along the first couple of hundred miles of roads, tracks and uncharted mud flats. We had compasses, and could see the distant line of the highlands, so we knew we were headed in the right direction. The vehicles held up well; there was a fuel dump for us at the foot of the highland slopes; the three girls were holding up well – together. They scarcely spoke, 'They're very animated with each other,' Prof commented. 'Weird little cabal.'

The two guys bailed out when we reached Morhora Ridge, overlooking the lake. They pointed to the distant promontory where we were to set up camp – a wide, sandy tongue sticking into the pale blue water. The whole broad, open valley looked fantastic in the slight haze – none of the mud we'd left behind. Prof must have known the twosome wasn't staying with us. He merely stared and nodded, and pointed me towards the driver's seat.

Mitch and Bmonga stayed on the ridge. 'We're walking the high trail,' they said. 'Bmonga's village is three days *that* way. We'll stay there for a couple of months.' And off they went, hand-in-hand, without a backward glance.

Fine, they're as much social company as the girls. None. I climbed into the Land Rover and started down the slope, with the girls staying together in the following vehicle. We made it mid-afternoon, and had the tents erected by dark.

Prof – three times my age – was the only sensible company to chat with, and, finally, when we had a fire going, and food barbecuing, he filled us in with a few more details. The essence of it was, 'The unidentified birds are still unidentified.' That was about it. 'So this is a great opportunity for me… us.'

I was thinking, 'Big Deal – so they're probably budgies with Men-in-Black glasses, pretending to be canaries.' And I could see myself being at Mount Ngoro goro very soon – the lava lake had even overflowed the caldera, and was intermittently spitting lava fountains a thousand feet into the air – much more my kind of raison d'être. Or raison de mourire, perhaps.

But I don't do deserting, and I liked Prof in a shittily antagonistic sort of way. Besides, I'd found myself quite interested – he'd been educating me all the way so far. The girls knew it all, anyway – doing their Ph.Ds under him.

So, next morning, after a ceremony with the local chief and a load of villagers from Godalone-knows-what-it's-called, we went up a low hill near the promontory so we could get the layout of the lake and the colony's distribution. It wasn't so much a low hill as an old dune, and the promontory was merely a low-lying spit of sand that intruded into the lake towards a low island. We did a quick survey of types that were expected to be there; gained a rough idea of numbers; telephoto lenses on anything especially interesting. I manned the cameras while the girls did the IDs and notes. And Prof paced round self-stimming, waving round and muttering.

Oh, bugger, I thought, *if you're going autistic on me, I'm definitely not stopping. I'll have a better chance up Ngoro.*

Watching them, every collection of birds seemed to move differently from others the same size, as well as being of various pastel shades, like the pelicans and flamingos. Mind you, if anything was different, it was the flamingos with their upside-down heads in the water. The small family group of ostrich was unusual, too. Even I knew that from my week's nose-burying… and there was a scatter of shoebills only fifty metres down the slope at the water's edge.

What took Prof's attention was the group of wading birds half a mile away, a white-silvery bunch. 'Just about a hundred,' I estimated from my five counts through the telephotos.

To my little-learned eye, they looked the same as the greater flamingos… different colour to the smaller pink ones, though. When I blew them up on the laptop, however, 'You're right, Prof, they do look different.'

'Of course they do, Peters. Why do I bother with you?'

I gave him my direst hate-mate look and carried on regardless, 'The wings look as if they have fingers half-way down, like pterodactyls—'

'And the legs have a bend too many,' Greta said.

'I thought they looked peculiar in their movements,' I said

'They fly like bats,' Ilse said.

'They're not birds.' Fenna said.

'See? They bend down, and grab for shrimps?'

'Yes, rather than beak-stab for it.'

'They're ficken fast at it,' Ilse ended the discussion.

That was it, Full Day One. Almost. We ate and talked as never in the previous weeks. *They* all became excited, anyway, and I listened to the radio for updates on whatever – Mount Ngoro goro had erupted violently in a massive series of explosions. 'Can't have been that massive – we never heard a thing.'

'The wind's been heading this way,' we calculated. 'There'll be fumes and ash, at least.'

'It'll totally destroy the lake… all the lakes… poison the shrimps and birds.' Prof was in his first-on-the-autistic-spectrum pacing round mode. Almost distraught.

The head guy from the village paid us a visit. 'Rebel militia groups have been seen at Lake Mkiri. That is next lake along the valley. They come this direction. Maybe we leave tomorrow. And also,' he shuffled his assegai from one hand to the other. 'You had two companions with you? Yes? They were observed by rebel group along the ridge where they rested for night, and were killed in traditional manner. They were seen to be, er,' he peered into the sky for memory of the quotation, '"in the abomination of sodomy together". It is forbidden by the church as well as the law. You two don't... er?'

'No, we bloody don't,' I looked at Prof in the same tone he was looking at me.

The three girls shuffled, looked shifty, conferred. 'We aren't prepared to remain.' And they took their leave in one of the Land Rovers at dawn.

'I'm staying,' I said. 'The conversation'll improve now there's just the two of us, and there'll be more food.' Fat chance with the conversation – his autistic mutterings were increasing. *Besides, so what if they come up here? What was that Odyssey song? If You're Looking for a Way Out?*

Three mornings later, two villagers arrived with news of an advance band of rebel soldiers at the far end of the lake – about six miles away. 'Your Land Rover will be taken if you remain. And the cameras, food, your computer. The marauders can sell anything, including you; hostages.' The look on their faces didn't indicate optimism for a high asking price.

'Not the best news, but what about you? The other villagers?'

They shrugged. 'Maybe…' one drew a finger across his throat. 'But we two stay, see who comes.'

We asked about the unusual birds. 'They arrived several years ago. There are more now. We never managed to catch any – for food.'

'These birds not have feathers.'

Ones they'd found along the lakeshore were more like long scales with fine fringes.

They returned to their village, and we stayed on the lakeside in the stifling heat and humidity, trying to sneak up on the bendy-leg non-birds. But every time we came close, they retreated to the low island beyond the sandspit. And stood there, waiting us out.

That was when the first of the grey ash began to settle – like fine sand that was sharp and prickly in your hands. We hadn't noticed the cloud drifting over from behind us – it wasn't too dense at first.

Highly undecided for a time – to flee or stay? We realised the vehicle wouldn't like the ash in the air, and it would screw up the engine. So we hid the cameras and laptop bag, and as much food as we could carry. 'What we came here for, Peters,' Prof said, looking along the lakeside, 'is the bendy-leg non-birds. And I'm not leaving without one.'

'You go,' I said. 'Get yourself safe in the Land Rover with all the data and scales samples.'

He hit me. Called me a traitorous thieving shit who wanted all the glory. Course, I pushed him off and he ranted more and got fixated on Peters the Glory-grabbing Git.

'Piss off, Prof.' I shoved him away. 'You sleep in the tent. I'm okay out here.'

'I'm keeping the keys,' he warned me.

‘I’m going nowhere. And you should be in the tent, not breathing this ash. It’s bad for your lungs. You sound rough enough already. Crotchety toerag.’

We did get close to the Bendies, maybe a hundred metres away, but they knew we were there, and shuffled away. That seemed to be their comfort distance. The photos were good, detailed, but still not sufficient for Prof. Or me, even with the university’s Lumix 60x zoom plus double-convertor. The heat-haze and the airborne ash and dust put paid to really crisp shots. We tried to surround them, sneak up and cut them off, but they were wise to it all and retreated to their safe little island.

Keeping the tent low and half-hidden, and the cameras and stores behind rocks not too far away, we hoped that if the rebels or government forces arrived, they wouldn’t get everything.

The Land Rover was a bit big to keep discrete, and Prof insisted on keeping it close by. We rowed about that – even came to blows again. But I wasn’t serious, and he had the keys, so we both stayed, and so did the Land Rover, but not for long.

It was a bad day, that Monday. The three girls were supposed to have messaged us before dusk, and didn’t. Prof coughed some blood up. And I had a drop-fit and almost drowned, being knee-deep in the lake at the time. My third in a week. Sure enough, we had a gang of rebels in tatty camouflage uniform surrounding us before sundown – all boots and AKs, Marmite skin and white teeth.

'You gave up the keys quick enough then, Prof,' I laughed. They broke into the food crates, and scattered the contents in disgust. Threatened the two of us, but left us alone after they'd slashed our tent in irritation at hearing of government troops coming this way. It probably wouldn't help their cause to have a pair of pallid bodies to their name.

'So we're stuck here now. Without the vehicle.'

'Not necessarily,' he had his thin little smile. 'The Aruna Department of the Interior knows we're here, and it would be bad publicity if we were stranded here. The arrangement was for them to check on us end of August. We only need to survive.'

So we stayed – too far to walk, anyway, especially with not being able to carry stores. And neither of us feeling so great. So we did what we came for – study the Bendy-legs.

'Definitely not birds.' Prof was convinced. 'The feathers we've found aren't true vaned feathers, they're proto-scales that evolved in a very different direction.'

'Those fingers on their wings extend a lot longer than we first thought…'

'And they're very flexible…'

'Certainly adept at picking and manipulating things.'

'Entirely new clade of reptile birds.' He was getting excited, for a Prof, and began thinking of Latin names for them that centred around bendy legs and his own name.

Patchily, the ash was drifting in, darkening the sky some days. Other days, a beneficent wind would take it elsewhere. But Prof was getting it on his chest – made worse because he wouldn't wear a dust scarf across his face. He coughed and gasped and spat and yargghhhhed and bled and died one morning, leaving his pillow and sleeping bag sluiced in slimy, ash-speckled blood. And me wondering what the blue Nora to do next.

My only real choice was to take a few photos of him as proof, bury him with a chitin non-feather, and wait for the Department of the Interior to arrive before I starved or died of thirst or ash. With sodall else to do, I watched the non-bird things until the usual pair of village visitors came over. 'A Land Rover has been seen. Its roof. In the mudflats.'

'Oh, well, exit a few thieving rebels.'

'No. It is your other vehicle, the one your friend ladies took. No-one came out of the mud.'

Oh dear. Just me then. Well, I suppose it's what I came for – one last adventure before this brain tumour gets me. Always knew New Zealand was a non-starter. Doubt I could get as far as Ngoro goro now, much less NZ. Best not wade too deep after the Bendies, I suppose. Although... it'd be one easy way.

I part-repaired the tent, tried to send messages and reports out on the net but I didn't know if anything was getting through, despite a couple of hundred quids' worth of solar-powered battery chargers.

Shuffling round, carting cameras, snap-pack and notebooks, I wasn't scaring the Bendies off as much as we both used to, and I managed to sneak closer – maybe thirty metres. When I managed that, I always sat and let them get used to me, or put up a diddy wind-break to hide behind. And they'd forget I was there, and wander closer where I could see them all in their fantasticness. Their beaks were semi-flexible, and made modulated sounds, which meant, I thought, they were communicating together in complex speech patterns. They collected shrimps and whatever else and slipped most of them into a belly pouch like kangaroos have. As dusk fell, they'd go for a fly round in a few circles before settling on the island in the near-dark.

'Checking up on the surroundings? Or just a wing-stretch?' I wondered, and stayed and watched through the whole of one night, and there weren't any around pre-dawn. I watched and wandered back and forth. 'Ah, here they come. Shuffling round.' They paddled en masse along the still, calm water margin with the sunup, but I'd swear they weren't on the island overnight, and the reed beds weren't thick enough to hide them.

My drop-fits were getting more frequent, and I was being a bit more careful about being in the water, or leaning over the fire. But for four months I'd known it was inoperable, hence the invented row with Mairaid, and the thought of seeing Ngoro goro erupting really close up. Really close up. One first and last time.

The ash was becoming deeper, but the reed growth seemed to keep pace with it, though I didn't see the blush of prawn pink on the water so intensely any longer.

Must be the end of August; government's supposed to send someone to look for us, aren't they? But I'm not going to last much longer on so little food, with so little variety. But nothing hurts particularly, so I might as well stay here in the tent. I'm practically among them at the tip of the sandspit, opposite their little island.

They actually took to coming all round me and looking at me, and peering in the tent. I swear they gibbered and jabbered among themselves about me and the gear. We even made a game of it, and I weirdly made sounds back at them. It was genuinely entertaining – for me, anyway. I'd make questioning sort of sounds, and they'd come up with what I imagined were responses, just like I used to with our old ginger cat – had some right conversations going with him at times.

Yeah, I'm not going far, am I? Couple of hundred metres would be my maximum distance walking, so when I heard the sounds of gunfire along the lake shore, a mile or two away, I didn't get into panic mode.

The Bendies seemed more troubled than I was, trotting round in flustered circles, some of them heading back to their island by water or flight. 'Pity. Are you going?' I sat and looked at them, the usual half-dozen – I knew their tiny differences by then – Tongo, Rangy and Whitey… Rupey, Tara and Wera. Made a few silly asking sounds, and sad sounds to say I'd miss them, and they were doing them back and poking at me with their beaky mouths. One actually touched me!

Voices much closer, a few hundred metres. I stood up to see. Jungle-camouflaged people – mostly men – swaggering this way, loud, waving their weapons. A few scattered shots. A burst of automatic fire.

My new friends were agitated, more of them taking off and circling away. More shots. They spread wider. My close bunch jabbered and poked and pushed at me, thigh- and waist-height. Herding me towards the water.

I stepped in, quite imagining that I'd be face-down and gone at the first sign of a tumour-inspired drop-fit. But they pushed and flapped and screeched me towards their island. The water immediately around it was shuddering in masses of vibration waves, as though the whole island was trembling.

Almost waist-deep in places, I was stumbling and floundering, hearing another couple of shots, and only just managing to get onto the smooth sandy shore. And it was! The island was vibrating, like a motor humming, very low, warming up. 'Oh, shit,' I said. 'You *are* bloody aliens.' Like the notion had been pin-pricking at the back of my mind for days.

The Bendies are vanishing in a long stream of pseudo-feathers into the steep face of what seems for all the world like a sand dune island. They're going through a space with a screen or something over it. I can't see past it, or inside, but they're all slipping through as though there's nothing there. *An entrance to…? Something vast and island-shaped? That hummed?*

Hear a couple more shots. I'm being motioned and beckoned towards it. Ten metres away, 'Go in there? Yes, not half. In my state. Nowt to lose, I'm game for anyth—' Hard slam in my back. Rammed forward. I'm down. Face into the hard sand, still conscious – not a drop fit. Can hear gunfire again. Deep pain, left side at kidney level.

I been shot.

Can't move, I'm twitching, 's all going dark.

'Buggerit.'

***

MANSFIELD WILL NEVER BE THE SAME AGAIN

I don't get gob-smacked by much I see in Mansfield. But this? Well, the place is never going to be the same.

Going round the market, minding my own business, as you do, and there it suddenly was: massive, like ten storeys high, and wide as a house. A slug. It looked just like a slug, anyroad: gigantic, it filled a whole corner of the marketplace, all rounded and organic-looking. Like slimy and throbbing. Yes, I know – I seen people like that, too.

So I'm standing there, mouth wide open, looking up at it, all shiny and oozy – the thing, not me. It suddenly sends tentacles flashing down, like tendrils. So fast. And it's grabbing someone and lifting him up, like examining them. All these arrays of sensors popping up in patches across its surface. And it's pulsing like an elephant's heart. Then it's starting to pull him apart and he's screaming and struggling. Not for long, though, poor sod. The brighter ones among us are doing an about-turn and legging it – get some distance between us, tucking in behind columns and in shop doorways.

Some, however, just don't believe it – you know how some folks are – and they're just standing there gawping.

Next, it's sending a great long tentacle-thing out and grabbing one of the women standing there… and a few more, as well. And it's got its tentacles all over'em – typical Mansfield. And it's stripping'em; and it starts dismembering them. Some others, it's stretching or crushing; twisting them up, like wringing them. Like it's doing torque-tests on'em. I can see all this blood splurting and bursting out. And it's shaking them as if to see if there's anything loose inside – like got a screw loose. It's getting fed up then, cos it's just dropping them. Some of the lumps on the exterior starts moving, and swelling. And they go in rotation all round it, like eyes switching on and searching.

Then, all of a sudden, it's shrinking down and swelling out sideways and longways, so it's looking even more like a slug, and it slid and slurped across the pedestrian precinct. No people there by then, and it's re-raising itself up the side of Marks & Spencers. These like tendril things are flickering in through the windows, bringing people out, holding them for a moment – some shrieking and struggling. Then it just drops'em to the pavement. One or two, it's chucking away, as if in disgust. I know how it feels, when I look round Mansfield sometimes. A couple of market stalls went flying – cabbages everywhere.

The big office and council building next to Marks starts falling apart. I can't see anything of what it's doing from where I am, but there's these great sections of the frontage coming tumbling outwards and collapsing, and I'm seeing all these people amongst the masonry and girders and dust coming up in great clouds.

Out on the streets, everybody's running back, of course, most screaming and dragging kids. A few are stopping to watch a hundred yards away, like they've reached their own feel-safe distance.

Everybody where I'm hiding is suddenly in a panic, because it's heading this way. I'm getting knocked over in the rush and next thing I know, it's right on top of me, overlapping me with its great rounded bulk. Bloody hell – it's really slimy close up, and stinks like compost. It's moving like a caterpillar, with the front stretching out and then the insides come slurping forward inside it. Then the back end sucks into it – it's revolting. It must have had its attention on the Bentinck memorial spire because it oozed across the square and stretched right up it. It's a really complicated steeple with four corner spires round the high main one. Or it was, anyway. This slug-thing's leaning right up there, hugging the whole spire, and sending its tendrilly tentacles all up them, pulling them apart as if they're nothing.

A guy near me's saying, 'The television people ought to be here. I'm going to sell my phone footage to Sky TV.'

Some religious nut woman decides she's going to talk to it or something, and she's walking towards it, praying really loudly and calling it a demon. It was, too. It demoned her alright, all over the market place. It hardly seemed to touch her – she must have hit a raw nerve with her screechy praying.

By then, there's me and this bald guy who's covered in tattoos keeping out the way in the doorway to the Four Roses Shopping Centre. 'Somebody ought to get the negotiators in from Lambeth.' And he's wanting experts from Cambridge or some such dreaming place. He was another nutter-type trying to contact it, and wanting to study it.

I said, 'I wonder where the nearest tanks are? Do we have reserve army units down at Chilwell or Kegworth or somewhere? We don't have Apache helicopters, do we? Cruise missiles?

Then the police arrived and two of them unrolled their stripy red and white tape to cordon off the area and keep it in. ‘Cordon it off with stripy tape?’ I said. ‘It’s fifty feet high, you berk.’

The big Officer Fuzz was a bit cross with me for saying that. ‘Get the other side of the tape where it’s safe,’ he ordered me. ‘Both of you, go inside the shopping centre.’ That was the last thing he did: a tendril wrapped round him. It took a tenth of a second, just long enough for him to look surprised. And he’d gone; leaving a great long red and white ribbon fluttering behind him. He should have let go.

The thing suddenly disappeared. Potwór ślimak, I called it. That’s what my Polish girlfriend calls her big fat dad. It had vanished.

Bald Tattoo said he thought it had zipped down to nothing – like squeezing itself into a cardboard box, and then that vanished. So he reckoned, anyway. But he’s from Mansfield…

‘Honest, Boss,’ Menolyptus Vee wasn’t really surprised to see his boss come slithering into his office just before prinkle time. ‘I simply popped out to some planet that was just put up on the “Unprotected” list. It was on the official bulletins this morning, right down near the bottom of the routine list. No details about it, so I thought, “I got nothing else on, especially.” So I went down on the off-chance, just to suss it out, to see if it was suitable, you know, for vacations. It could be the next place to start pushing to the punters. We need a fresh angle: somewhere new to keep the customers happy and paying, huh?'

'And is it suitable?' Heggidorphyn sent querying pulses.

'Yes, could be.' Menolyptus Vee shrugged his elbagoyles. 'But we'd have to plan how to pitch it. The place is full of these little ant creatures. They're busy, and scurry and squeak and have lots of constructions. Everything's a bit fragile, though: I crunched a few of their erections in a cluster, like a Xerotype hive, it was.'

'What do they taste like? Any good?'

'They stick in the teeth a bit; the outer covering's a touch leathery, but if you get that off, they're not bad.'

'Maybe an acquired taste? Could we make up some ideas of local dishes? A few head parts sticking out of pies or something of that nature? Maybe take a few pots of various flavoured dips to try them in first?'

'I was thinking, Boss: we could trade on the freaky adventure angle more than local dining. We'd have to theme it in the adverts, something like, "Panic makers and lovers – come and create havoc." You know, have a bit of wreck and ruin. Fun days. Not too much or too often, or the planet couldn't keep up and rebuild as fast as we destroy. We'd need to make it expensive, limited to a few visitors per diurn, with no weaponry allowed. Make it all sklids-on stuff, up close and personal. I pulled a few apart myself with no trouble. It's easy. They squeak as they lose bits. Don't take to being screw-twisted very well, either.'

'So we'd need to set a demand-pricing-sustainability balance, then?'

‘I reckon so; start very high and exclusive, advertise it as a “must-have” for the rich.’

‘Defensive capability?’

‘None that I detected, although I was only there one sustera. That might be long enough to pitch the visits at, in case they do have other systems lurking in reserve.’

‘So we could market the risk element, too. There’s a come-on lure I know to boost that idea.’

‘You’re prepared to give it a go, then Heggy? Visit the place yourself?’

‘Well, sounds like we could be on another winner with this one, eh, Meno?’

‘Yep – let’s shake and shoon on it, eh?’

‘And shlurt all over it, huh?’ They laughed, elly-ectitiously.

MY INSENSIBLE FINGERS

'You!' I looked up. The bark was directed at me. 'Humani male Sincer. You are the guilty person. Stand at once.'

What? I'm in complete blank shock. I stood, stomach suddenly very drained, legs a-wobble. What have I done? Nothing I know of. Certainly not to attract the attention of the Security Squad. They're Humanics, yes, but in uniforms and coverings that hid their actual origin – Humani or Homid. It saved accusations of bias, in theory. Either way, they act like neutereds, like machines. Their appearance here at the social club was a deep shock to me… to all of us, judging by the stilled silence all around. The SS officers simply aren't seen around, especially not in a place like this.

That night was just another event. Genuinely, it was good. It was enjoyable and fascinating. So revealing about ourselves, as well as them, the homids. And I'd been making loops of notes about everything I concluded, or wondered about.

'Someone,' The senior SS Uniform stated, his eye-pieces staring at me, 'has inserted a series of illegal codes into one of the link-pads. It has completely wiped the whole database for the community – financial, communications, stores, records, legal and personal. The continuation of the whole community is jeopardised. This is a deliberate, vindictive act of sabotage.'

I glanced round. All eyes accusing me. It had been stated; therefore, I am guilty.

Escorted out, to my profound embarrassment and shame, they took me to a cell-block I didn't know existed. 'We traced the infarctoid to a console that you used.'

'Yesss…' I admitted that readily enough – there'd be my log-on details and everything. 'I was exploring some aspects of higher moral thinking modes with one of the homids, Elseen.'

We were sort-of friends, Elseen and I; been doing things together for the past three dozen days – we seemed to naturally gravitate together – mutual liking, I suppose. There was never one hundred percent common ground between humani and the homids, but I was increasingly feeling that we were heading that way. I certainly liked her, which made it supremely interesting for my general awareness-raising of my own thinking and moral beliefs, as well as hers. Same as me, she must be a representative of her people, with some kind of brief to discover what she could about us. That was the basic point of the whole of the community, after all. I'd gained so many insights into her thinking patterns and motives, reasoning… so much so that I was lost in the mass of contradictions, much as she must be with me.

The homids are incapable of being untruthful. She had, in another room, denied all knowledge of anything. I veered towards the link being hacked. But the SS had it sussed: 'No hacking. It must have been one of you. It could not have been her – she is incapable of lying. Ergo – You.'

They weren't interested in why I might have done it – 'Bored? Not going your way? Want to run a group test? Who cares why?'

* ✳ *

I received the punishment. Quite summarily. And severely. Presumably because the potential damage was enormous; and I wouldn't admit it. They were very keen on always being truthful. I clearly wasn't, and should thus be given a salutary lesson.

'Elseen will know I did nothing – she was with me.'

'She agrees that she saw nothing.'

'So I—'

'Must have done it when she wasn't attending to the details of your every input.'

* ✳ *

Brutality as I've never experienced: forcibly stripped. I did resist, ineffectually, and bruisingly, though I didn't notice the bruises when it was over. Six lectro-bolts. Mind-blasting and body-scorching. I had no idea that such inhumanity existed, or such pain.

I was allowed to dress, but couldn't move – every joint a mass of stiffened agony; every thought was one of black, disbelieving horror.

Early the following morning, they came. 'Not worth dressing you merely to walk back to the punishment cell.'

I took the same lectros. Six more. I noticed the burning smell. The crisped hairs on my body. The near-bursting eyes. Being carried back to the other cell. 'How many?' I tried to ask; just a croak. 'How long?' It was unheard.

* ✶ *

Six days. Time to recover my breathing between each. Time to weep and curse. Time to think. Not about my guilt or whatever – I didn't believe this could happen in our civilised two-peoples settlement.

No, it was more a matter of letting my mind drift over the project, and the sixty or seventy days since the community was set up – I lost count somewhere in the pain and shock. The project had seemed so exciting – not dangerous at all – but refreshing to be involved in something like that. Thirty of us humani had volunteered to join in the informal getting-to-know-you exercise with the homids.

Both groups had begun to colonise the planet forty-odd years ago, and lived fairly distantly without conflict when we did encounter each other. Our languages were both traceable to early human expansion. Our ancestors had spread in different directions – stellographically, physically and mentally. And here, for the first time in countless millennia, we had met again – from opposing directions.

There didn't seem to be great distrust between us, so much as unknowingness. Perhaps each group was afraid that the others had become more than them over the countless millennia. Different, yes, obviously. In what ways? Superior to us? Do they have the same fear? Wariness of us? They must have.

Thus, the powers had come up with this Two-Peoples Project idea – low key, almost a commune, the first where humani and homids were mixing freely together. Some working together, though none living with each other, not in partner-pairs, anyway. Experiments of some undisclosed nature had indicated that we could no longer interbreed, and thus we aren't even the same species now. Someone must have wanted to find out, I suppose. You'd think DNhA would provide all kinds of answers, but that's not my area.

I'm a non-specialist, whereas most of the other volunteers had a brief to look for specific aspects – intelligence markers, effects of physical differences, and language traits, particularly. I was more on the general worker side – bit of organisation, provisions, social events; and keeping an overall eye on anything and everything. Pulling things together, I suppose, or seeing what aspects of both peoples linked themselves together. I'm sociable, so I've been arranging social events, looking for topics to engage both groups in, and not just sit and twiddle our thumbles and thumblings.

Painting, dancing, gardening, all the usual ideas. Along with some rambling, climbing, swimming; and games for individual challenges, and team sports. Plus vids, televees, corders and V games. Personally, I found the drinks nights the most socially mixing, almost regardless of the topic – table games, IQ, logic and knowledge contests, or just chattering afterwards – getting philosophical, or maybe argumentative.

Mmm, such occasions were quite revealing, I thought, about their attitudes to us, to life, freedom and authority; our misconceptions about them; modes of logic, ethics, higher beliefs…

* ✳ *

Six days later, I had no work to go back to when I was permitted to leave. The cell door was open. Someone waved me out. The few people I saw, of either population, looked the other way as I made my determined-not-to-limp way to wherever it was that I lived… oh yes… the single storey cabin with the clump of pinooka trees providing shade, 'Just what I need,' I thought. 'Some shade from all this.'

I sat on my tiny terrace, a few gleam-beetles edging close in case of titbits. I categorically needed to drink. Lots. Strong. Spread over the whole of the coming day. Flagons and flasks of whatever I happened to have in. As Social Guy Number One, I had plenty in. And I sat on the most padded lounger in the patchy, intermittent shade and burning sun. And sipped, and blurred my way into the postnoon, tossing occasional biscuits or nibbs to the beetles. Quite courageous, some of them. Almost came up begging like a miniature terrahound.

I took consolation in their presence and their actions; a diversion from the pain and deep, deep ache. No more thinking on the reasons, or what I would do over the looming days. Just the drink and green-gleaming beetles – fascinating little things. Organised and very beautiful…

The drink, whatever it was, was so soothing to body and mind. A little more perhaps? I offered myself. Do you want some? No – the Gleam Beetles didn't drink; they even turned their proboscises up at a grape-spirit we produced nearby – the Twa-Valley Reserve.

* ✳ *

'Hello.' It was towards dusk – sun had gone. Still some light, red-violet tinged. Elseen. I didn't move – too much effort and pain to re-crack my joints before I had to. Besides, I was moderately certain that I was stuck to the padding.

‘How are you?’

I had not the slightest idea how to respond. Somehow, it hadn’t occurred to me that I would ever see her again. She came in front of me, scattering my beetle ensemble. I vaguely wished she hadn’t, and almost lost my grip on my glass as I refilled it.

‘May I sit?’

I waved, ‘Chairs are over there; bring one round. I’m not moving.’ I doubted I could move. Stiffened and caked into the lounge-chair’s padding. I’d felt the blood oozing since mid-afters when I went for a pee over the end of the terrace. I hoped it didn’t sound like I was being deliberately impolite, but I was too far gone to care.

She put a chair next to me, so we could both watch the slowly fading light, ‘I’m sorry about what happened to you.’

I managed half a chuckle – a chuck, I suppose. ‘Me too. Drink? Glasses inside – help yourself. I’m not moving for days.’

‘I’m sorry. It was an experiment. We are incapable of being untruthful. I have undertaken some conditioning to see if I could be mendacious, even when there were consequences, severe consequences.’

‘There weren’t any consequences. Not for you. What did you do? Did you see someone—?’

‘I did it. I had pre-programmed one three-key code to initiate a sequence. Self-deleting. Undetectable. One touch was all I needed.’

‘You, hmm?’ I looked at her, couldn’t link the shock of that night and the six days of screaming racking pain, with her, with Elseen. It wasn’t in her nature. She was pleasant, very likeable, honest, bright. Not a liar. It was unthinkable for a homid to lie –they can't.

She gazed at me. Don't know if she wanted forgiveness or what. I almost put the glass down, but I'd never find it again if I did, 'Why would you?' I tried to delve her possible reasons, decided it was impossible as I saw her for what she was, an alien. Her mind operates on a different reasoning plane, 'I thought we had some measure of mutual understanding—'

'No. You're only a humani; you're incapable of the kind of higher reasoning and philosophising that characterise we homids.'

My eyes ached. They had for days. They wept on their own some days of late. Just leaking. Like the open burns across my back. Couldn't look at her.

'Do you hate me?'

I wondered. Do I? I ought to. Maybe I did, a dead sort of hate. More, perhaps, disappointment, because she scorned us, despised me. When I thought we had begun to be friends.

She stared into my eyes, waiting for an answer. 'We wanted to see if we could be untruthful, even in the face of significant costs. Normally, it is entirely inconceivable for us to do such a thing.'

Us too, to that extent, I thought. *Not to bring that onto someone, merely to test a thought. Do you have any idea how much pain? how bad it was?*

I thought I'd seen within her in those days before. But she was inscrutable now – a blank. *You're a nothingness, Elseen. To do that and think you're superior?* I'd really thought we might… whatever. My spine and every joint stung with the memory of raging after-pains of the punishment that she had deliberately put me in for.

Her misdemeanour, not mine, for the sake of a simple test on herself. My agony, not hers. She'd had it all worked out. She was intelligent and bright; at times solemn and thoughtful. Was it truly a mere experiment? To know something about themselves? Or wanting to understand us? Part of some personal drive, or a whole-group mission?

Fleetingly, it crossed my mind that they could have been testing me to make me want to be part of them? To step up to their philosophy and thinking level? Become super-humans?

To the Hells and Bells of Sebatta with that; they're no super-thinkers any more than we are, I finished a drink and carefully poured another. 'Hate you? No. You're beneath that. Not worth my effort. I'll get over this eventually. But will you? Have you destroyed yourself? And reduced your people? Unless you have courage, and go back there, confess, and suffer your just deserts?' I waited for a response. 'No?'

She looked even more blank-eyed than always. *Well may you look like that,* Elseen, *I thought, you've opened the airlock to a whole ne was of thinking and behaving. You deliberately conditioned yourself to lie. Such a terrible slippery slope you've stepped on.*

I sipped, thinking, *I need another pee, so why don't you just go?*

'No? You're not up to confession? So stay lower than we are. I'm more than that – I'd go and admit it. And that makes me more than you.' I attempted to shrug, half lying there.

I didn't really notice when she left.

* * *

Sometime, I woke up, the long-stem glass dangling in my insensible fingers. ‘Need to finish my report…’

Such a huge effort to uncrack myself from the lounger, rise and totter to a keyboard. “This community experiment has been most successful. The homids,” I dotted down, “are devious, lying, cheating creatures. They are too much like we humani for either group to be awe or fear of the other. We’re all so much the same that we should simply treat them as we do ourselves. They are taking giant steps to become much as we are.”

OPTION THREE.

My conchiglie partner's shell has suddenly begun to thicken up. 'Winter's coming, Rod,' she told me. 'First day of Autumn.'

'Huh?' I looked around – a rocky high-mountain slope, all our drilling and sample-mining equipment scattered across our camp.

'I need to get down in the lowlands,' she said. 'Season's over.'

'You can't. Not just like that. What about all this lot?'

'We can pack it in the wagon. It will take me a day or two to create my hibernation shell.'

'You never told me this happened. Can't you delay it?'

She shrugged, with slight cracking sounds from her thickening shell. 'We can get down to a cabin on Four-Thou level where there's a small trading post. We can over-winter there.'

'Over-winter? Great,' I was flummered. 'Now you tell me. I thought we were out here—'

She was already packing the trailer. '…for another fifteen days? And then over-wintering all the way down in Florritown? No?' Apparently not – she started the wagon's T6 motor and pointed the cumbersome vehicle down the bare slope, just as the first swirls of snow whipped around me. I climbed in, not a second too soon, as she gunned the engine a couple of times and headed down the whitening slope. Flummering aliens.

The cabin was there, alright, but it wasn't merely the single little refuge cabin she had spoken of, tucked against a rockface with a scarcely-snowproof roof. This was much bigger, a very solidly built trading post with overnight rooms for summer visitors. A youngish man ran the place, a mixture of world-weary and twinkle-eyed, welcoming us into the polished and warm-lit entrance area. A real fire. A blast of heat! This was Total Amazement.

'You're only just in time,' he said, 'She's shelling up rapidly. You'll definitely have to stay here. She'll be OK. Some of them do it every year – I have five pre-paid shellies in the cellar dorm right now. They like to push the season as long as possible. Humans like you, and me, die of cold and starvation if we're caught outside in the mountains, but conchiglie simply go into deep freeze for the season, even outdoors.

'Drink? Sit awhile. My other human guest isn't here just now; you've plenty of time to warm up, have a drink, give me the latest gossip.'

That suited me, if only through sheer relief at not being caught outside for the winter – and so unexpectedly.

'The conchiglie can hibernate wherever they happen to be. Come the Spring melts, they wake up. If they had a human partner, they're almost certainly frozen solid and dead. Which seems to be the conchies' intention, because it leaves them inheriting the joint profits, with all the survey info and samples from the previous season.' He looked again at my partner, 'Not seen this one before. She must be new at it. Used to be a common thing with them, entrapping humans so they can double their profit.'

'So, I'm gonna starve here? Is the valley still open lower down?

'No – termination snowfall was three days ago. Valley's completely impassable till the melts.'

'Shuggs!'

'There is hope.' He gave me that faded look. He must practise it every day. 'I got caught that way one time. Near froze to death in a ravine. I covered a tight spot over with branches and tarp and hunkered down with my partner.'

'Yeah? What did you eat?'

'My partner. One hundred twenty days. Can't face conchi-meat even now.'

'But?'

'I built this place two years later. It's a crossroads between the long-valley route and the passes into Medan and Highgrass. I get the passing trade in summer; plus a few trappers in the winter; maybe a few guests staying over for a time in the snows.'

'You get people and conchis staying? Long period?'

'Sure. Like you. Ain't got any choice, unless you want to get off my property? Your partner there would survive outside, but she'll be more comfortable inside – less stiff when they thaw out. Mostly our guests are in similar pairs. I come to an arrangement.'

'Such as?' I had a sinky sort of feeling about this.

'Well, if it's a single conchiglie who just turns up, I check out their property and samples, and charge proportionately for their storage. If they've pre-booked, like the five down in the basement, it's a standard fee. Unless they've admitted they deliberately dumped their human partner somewhere higher up in the first-fall colds – to inherit the partnership.'

'And then?' He passed me another drink – warm and mulled.

'I wait till they've gone completely solid, and either crack'em open – some folks'll eat them even now – kind of an unusual dish. Or, I can store them indefinitely – there's an ice cave about a thousand ticks up the north face of Hielo Mount – *that* one.' He pointed straight up through the roof, towards the mountain the cabin complex was nestled against. 'It never thaws in the bottom. At the last count, I had around a dozen conchies piled up in there, not that I ever climb down to do an inventory.'

I was smack-faced. 'No? Really?'

'How else am I supposed to make a profit? I get folk like you want to eat all winter for free. Nothing's free. So I have to make a charge – thirty percent of your season's takings. That way, you come out alive, and your partner—'

'My partner? Yesss?'

'Comes out however you want – they're in full hibernation, so the choice isn't up them. Option 1: They wake up snug and smug in Spring. 2: They get split and roasted over a log fire at the Four-Roads Barbecue. Or 3: I roll them down the ice cave for the next thousand yonks – that's a free option, by the way. And you have two thirds of their profit, too.

'Flummery – I never thought. I mean, it takes some thinking about.'

‘Sure it does. Your partner’s not going to have any say in it – she’s shelled-up solid already. What do you think her motives actually were? Why don’t you chat it over tonight?’

‘Who with?’

‘My other guest. She arrived yesterday. I expect she’s in her room, recovering from her descent yesterday. She had a long drag down from Three Peak Lookout. Name’s Dyna. We’re actually booked to roll her partner down the ice cave tomorrow.

‘We can do hers and yours together if you decide on Option Three. Another drink?’

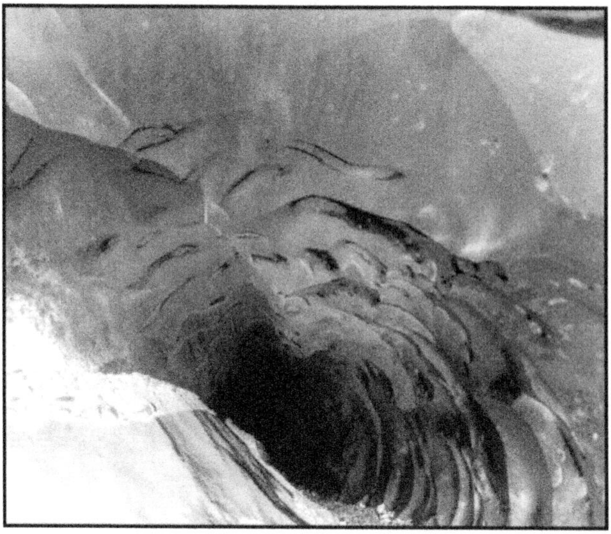

'Zockle! It's size of my home village. It'd take around an hour to walk from one side to the other.'

'It's ten times bigger than any other spacecraft I ever even heard of, much less actually seen.'

'Size ain't everything, not with spaceships.'

'Whatever, it's heading through our system, so they send us to run our facets over it.'

The five of us stood at the Stella Nova's external Panam screens and watched the all-encompassing displays. Being the regional patrol and survey ship, it was inevitable that we'd be sent to discover its intentions, "Find out where it it's from, Polly, and who or what's aboard; its heading and purpose. Anything, really.'

Looming vast in our screens as we approached, 'It's *enormous*.'

'And complex, like a cluster of techno stations fitted together.'

'Still silent. We're not picking up a whisper or a bleep on any device we have.'

Edging round the huge bulk in a spiral observation pattern, we couldn't discern any way in or out. 'Its drive isn't too clear, either. No power emissions – not exactly drifting at that speed, more like it reached cruise-speed and switched off.'

It hadn't been heading for us; there was a slight gravitational curve on its trajectory, but nothing overtly purposeful. Probably just passing through. Which could mean a variety of things: it was going somewhere? Or it was lost? Systems broken down? Crew and passengers long deceased?

The one very definite thing was that it had been traveling for centuries. At least.

Not threatening us, not strictly inside our inner space.

'But what is it?' I convened a meeting of the flight staff.

They shrugged collectively. 'Back-plotting doesn't tell us much. Seems to be from the direction of Mohab Cluster towards Galactic Centre?' *So Navigation Nathan isn't the big breakthrough I hoped for.*

'Maybe, but Mohab's a very dense star region. Thousands of possibles.'

'Could have been on exploratory mode? Changed course with every star it approached? Origin could be anywhere.'

'Species? Ideas?' I asked.

'No identifying markings. Could be any.'

'We always assume,' Ajo, our non-expert on anthropology, said, 'that passing or visiting craft are one of our Arach Empire vessels, or one of the Basic Friendlies species.'

'And we're familiar with all their usual designs…'

'But this one?' We studied the pathetic amount of data we'd managed to gather. '*This* is different from anything we've seen before.'

We circled it again, more slowly, closer in; we beamed lights, rads, high-V and beacons at it in 720 wave-styles. Even sent the interceptor launch in among the antennae and protrusions looking for a possible airlock ingress and egress point.

‘There’s a couple of maybes,’ Engines Petrina spiked back. ‘And a pod of four small craft in cradles.’

‘Still no sign of life,’ Ajo studied the screens closely, ‘or clue as to body-size and morph from peering in the mirrored ports, or the size of external laddering, whatever.’

‘We have to bear in mind that it’s moving through our solar system – we have a finite time with it here.’

We circled, vidded, analysed, pondered. ‘That’s definitely a pair of drive units – the two star-pattern exit units. They’re big enough to get a quad-craft into. Not a familiar design. Can’t make out any unit lettering or numbers.’

Knocking, beaming, sonicking, heat apps – coding the pads alongside the maybe airlocks. Nothing bore fruit.

‘Kluk! It just clicked.’ Engines Petrina was choking over the waves, waving out the monitoring screens from one of the possible airlocks. ‘I tried a simple 4-2 code. It’s come open.’

‘Do not enter that vessel on your own,’ I ordered her, but she waved without even turning round. ‘It looks deserted, Polly. I’ll be alright.’ Totally against my repeated command, she went in, even sealing the lock behind her. I told three of the others to get their stuff together, and be ready to come out with me on a rescue foray – expecting never to see her again.

The outer door irised open just as we approached in the shuttle pod. ‘Seems to be deserted,’ Petrina said when we assembled in the airlock. The door closed behind us. Oxy-mix hissed in. ‘It’s breathable,’ Petrina said. ‘I tried it for a moment or two. Walked both directions along here…'

A broad corridor stretched to left and right. Clean, dim-lighted for the first thirty or forty paces; a soft-plaz flooring – so their F-Grav was working – a species that perambulated, not floated or flew. 'Maybe the side panels are doors.'

'I tried a couple. Locked.'

'There's lettering, numbers on some of them.' We took pics and statted them back to the Stella Nova, then walked, cautiously, on tarsal tips; quietly. The place had a deserted air.

'Yo! Yo! Anyone here?' The sounds echoed back to us.

'What ya doing?'

'Trying not to surprise anyone or anything that might be lurking. Letting them know they have company.'

That seemed to make sense, so we took it in turns to shout inane phrases. We found some kind of small equipment at a corridor junction; more lettering. There was an open door, an empty room… some fixed equipment with no obvious purpose.

'It's so quiet,' Mygg noted, 'Makes me nervy.'

Of it does; medical pursers are always nervy about something.

'Probably a bit smaller creature than we are. That's not a language I recognise. Even the glyphs themselves don't look right. There's nothing in the equipment I recognise as being for any particular function.'

'Definitely an unknown species from the looks of everything.' Still we moved on – pic-clicking and statting, opening a few doors, shouting every minin or two, but there was no indication of purposes of rooms or direction to engines, stores, command centre or anywhere else.

So huge. The whole cavernous thing felt as though it should echo to our voices, but there was nothing – sound-deadening walls and floors all around. So eerie. So empty.

'I know it's not natural, anyway,' I said, 'but this thing feels totally *un*-natural, it's a void, so quiet.'

'Looks like it opens to a larger space ahead – assembly hall perhaps?' We went, less cautious than we had been – up on four legs. Simply not expecting there to be anything alive in the whole thing by then – a deserted craft, a derelict – one that still maintained its basic self-survival functions.

The first part of the open space may have been some kind of assembly area, but the far end – shrouded in darkness – was a mass of conduits and valves, processors and ladders filling the high end-wall. *Part of the enviro-control system*, I imagined. *Eerie.*

We moved ahead, suddenly more wary, more exposed.

'Stop! Stop stop.'

'What?'

'I thought I saw movement. Just a glimpse. Something caught my eye. Down there among the equipment.' We kept still, peered into the hall. Waited.

I called, 'Hi. Hello. Anyone there?'

'Nothing…'

It was disappointing. Or a relief. I wasn't sure which. I scrutinised the darker corners of the space, finding I was desperate to find something there. *Anything*. Ajo pulled the bag from his back and sorted through the contents. He pulled out the L-vis sensor, and began to scan the hall… slowly, letting it probe the massed machinery, pausing at any dark patch. Nothing… cool, dead.

'There! Look. See?' A sensor had flicked – registered something. Jacko held the imager steady, hoping for more.

We waited, speaking in whispers, 'Yes, *there*. Something alive.' I thought it might be too threatening to move forward – frighten whatever it was away. Ajo prepared a set of light patterns, and rigged up some sound sequences. Mygg set about trying to match the glyphs on some walls and doors with anything in our banks. There was nothing similar. She beamed pics of them back to our ship and requested further language information, any identification. Possible origin.

'There! Something's stepped out from the shadow.' It wasn't clear at that distance. Fifty paces perhaps. Two of them. Had to be aliens. Living ones. Standing there, unmoving, holding something white. One larger than the other. Both upright, but still only half our upright size. Obviously dressed in some kind of clothing. 'I presume that's a sensory unit at the top; almost spherical. Probably contains the brain,' Ajo whispered.

'That'll be a central multi-survival mass in the middle. Twin locomotion units below – only twin-jointed. The appendages holding the white thing must be for manipulation purposes.'

'That looks like a sheet of scribing plaz it's holding. The other one is a bit smaller; but the same basic design – a mass of fine tendrils hanging down from the upper unit.

'I'll edge towards them… real slow,' Jacko murmured. 'Call to them.'

'No, wait... they're coming this way.' And so they were, hesitantly, hugging the wall in the shadows. Small, perhaps timid. Until they reached a brighter-lit spot, and stopped under the light. One of them dropped the plaz sheet. Pausing just a moment, they backed away, retreating to the shadows once more.

Miggles went forward to look at it, 'Slowly, girl,' I said. Miggles is the smallest among us, and probably looks the least threatening – until you get to know her, of course. And she's the nippiest on her pads if she needs a fast retreat.

She was pretty good at retrieval, actually – slow and unthreatening, picking up the sheet, giving the slightest antennal wave into the shadows – she can be friendly like that – and easing herself back to us.

The card displayed a series of glyphs. 'A message?'

'Must be?'

'A threat?'

'Ordering us off their ship?'

A communal shrug later, and I statted the card, beamed it back to the Stella Nova, and waited for their Dax analysis. Studying the darkness for long minutes, there was no sign of the two small aliens in the impenetrable shadows. 'Must have been quite brave to risk coming within thirty paces of people like us – we're a good bit larger than they are.'

'They might regard us as invaders.'

It seemed like an age of waiting, until the statt pinged – a reply from the Stella Nova. It was an SSC – the standard species category form – little more than a technical tick list – *JayKwii's not being helpful again; awkward zockler.* The analyser on the Nova had highlighted one summary line out the hundred or so spectrals, glyph-types and wave forms. We touched a few buttons to translate it into UniStang that non-technos like me can understand. "Humanoid. Type 7.8. Original Terran Commonwealth," the summary said, plus four lines of binary code, followed by, "Metabolism 2ac1. TREX-78. NSS 23076. CE."

'Stuff my carapace!' Ajo muttered, ''They're humanoids – *humans.*'

'Never!' I looked at him; and checked the diagram and data on the info pad again. 'Ahh, there's something else coming through. JayKwii's added something. "I think the first part of their message pad translates as, *Hello.* And the rest seems to be *Who are you?"'*

'Let's have another look…' Jacko turned the readout around to see better, '"NSS 23076… That means Not Seen Since 23076."' He read out, '"Type 7.8 – Considered Extinct."'

'Eh? Extinct?' This was antenna-twisting and haemo-curdling awesome. I gazed back across the space. They were still there, half hiding behind a bulkhead and cylinder assembly. My hearts were beating a quickstep, *This is awesome – extinct aliens – humans – wow!* We looked through the Info-Pad for further data – Male and female reproduction, soft body, endoskeleton, fragile but moderately flexible. Believed to be…

I gazed across the hall where they lurked on the edge between dim light and deep gloom, seemingly afraid. *These little things are vestiges of pre-civilisation eras, fabled creatures… it's impossible.*

'Three of them now… four…'

'The new arrivals are larger.'

I checked. 'Live-bearers, not egg-layers. This is awesome. Could be adults and offspring.'

‘Do they carry diseases?’ Mygg asked.

I Daxed it, ‘Loads – but nothing to affect anyone else. Jipps – they’re the 69th most ancient species on the list, out of 71 – they’re *primaeval* – practically Originals. We’re looking at living fossils here.’

‘Sixty-ninth? *Never!* I’ll have to check,’ Ajo looked stone-head gone out, ‘but that must be about the oldest known by far – I thought forty-five was the furthest-back that still existed.’

‘They don’t look overly lively, do they?’ Jacko sniffed four nasals at once.

‘Probably terrified,’ I said. ‘As far as they’re concerned, we’re monstrous-sized trespassers. Haraeth-alone knows how long they’ve been aboard this vessel. They’ve never seen anyone before, outside their own craft. Their coverings don’t look super-smart, huh?’

‘Think they’re lost? Out of power… control?’

‘That’s what I’m thinking. Control gone, but must have some power, or the enviro wouldn’t be active.’

‘So what do we do?’

‘Statt back to JayKwii and get him to fill in a card with info about us. Translate it into the same language. Send it back to them?’

‘That could take ages,’ I said. ‘I’m not waiting days. Give me the message pad. I’ll jot something down and translate it into… what’s it called?’

Jacko checked, ‘Englo-Humanic.’

‘What?’ Ajo was aghast, ‘Are *you* going across to meet them? *You’ll* make First Contact?’

‘Someone has to.’ *Oh, yes, yes, yes, I zockling am. Nobody else gets this honour. Whatever risk there might be.* ‘I’ll write something.’ *But zockler! What should I write? Something not too technical or complicated. A simple greeting, perhaps?*

Carefully, I entered a message into the Dax-pad, and pressed for the translation to appear – in ancient Englo-Humanic. *Must be the first time anyone's had a real cause to write in that language for ten thousand years... fifty-thousand, more like.* Slowly, I lowered myself into forward transit mode; more like their height: *This is going to be the most delicate – and important – thing I ever do.*

Hoping, and praying to Haraeth that I'd translated the First Words right, and they were appropriate, I started towards the patch of light with our message. *History'll judge me. It'll have to do.*

Very slowly, I was getting closer, trying to keep as low as I could. *Don't intimidate them... or spark them into attacking us... or disappearing... Please... stay there...*

They held their ground, must have realised I didn't mean any harm. *Yes... they're humanoid.* The two smallest ones were closest, others behind in the shadows…

I stopped and glanced down at the message pad. Hoping I had the words right, I held it out, "Hi. I'm Polly. Are you okay? Can I help?"

The smallest alien… *human…* took the pad directly from my tenty-tips, and studied the words. It showed its companion. That one took it, looked for a moment, and poked at the sensipad. *It's writing a reply.* I hadn't imagined this far ahead…

It leaned the top part – the head – on one side, then held out the message pad for me. I wrapped a tip around it. Zockle! I was almost trembling with nerves.

I turned it round just as the words were translating into UniStang…

'Hello, Polly,' The message was appearing slowly. 'Do you have a kettle you can put on?'

SINGLE-USE

We've been lining up and manoeuvring round, edging and guessing where the Nemica might be placing themselves. You'd think in a place the size of a solar system, and with all our ranging-and-search gear, we could each locate the enemy without much effort. However, with baffles and vad interference… misinfo… altered imagery and data, we could be anywhere, and so could they.

But, one way or another, one of us is always going to find the other eventually, and let loose. Then both sides'll know where everybody else is. And there won't be anyone left – not Nemica or humans.

I'm coordination officer board the ESS Valiant. *Coordination?* That's the last thing I know anything about – no-one tells me anything. All the stuff coming down the waves is intercepted and filtered by our own officers and auto-systems. Not that Valiant is a massive WarVessel: we're a small run-and-hit craft. *Very* fast; extremely agile; lethal weaponry audit; and effall defence capability – except speed and agility.

We lodge in a bay that bulges out the skin of a Battlegroup Topweight, making it look as though the ship has picked up a nasty little ganglion. In an active situation, the idea is that the brass find out where the enemy is, and we're loosened from our bay – there are four of us, the fleet's total – they lost faith in the idea soon after they fitted us up. But, money spent has to be justified, so we're still deployed.

When we're loose, we stick close to the hull, like a little swarm of ariidae fish, held steady in the field grippers, poised outside as an option. If needed, we can be let off the leash, and sent in with half a dozen weapons systems programmed to turn on them. We like to think of ourselves as terriers with fangs, claws, whiptail, poison spit, fire-breath and spurs – all at great speed and torque. Not that the brass ever expresses much faith in us, 'Midgies like you? Y' like a cotton tripwire to catch a tank.' Commander Ridl told us at the boarding briefing. 'We won't be needing you, but you'll be deployed anyway.'

He has a great line in sneers.

So basically – Oh, I say "we" and "us". It's actually just me and my little ship, the ESS Valiant. It's like President Prachtig calling himself "we" in the sense of him and the Federation. Here, it's me and the Valiant. That equals "we". I'm the only person aboard, and my only job is to keep an eye on whatever's happening. Sure, I'm called the Coordination officer, but I only coordinate anything when we're cut loose, which has only happened three times, and we didn't do anything. The rest of the time, when we're lodged inside, the big ship coordinates directly with my little ship, and nobody knows what the fuck they talk about.

I suppose, with there being four Single-Use ships in the fleet, it's also "we" in the sense of me and the other three – a tiny clique all on our own.

Anyway, basically, if I'm launched, I'm in Amber Mode, and if I'm freed, I'm automatically in Attack Mode. Originally, there were three other crew aboard, operating the main consoles, sort of manually. But every time they were used, they jammed up and were mashed. So the Powers-that-be by-passed crew, and channelled everything through in-board systems, or the Topweight's systems. But that didn't pan out too well if the mother ship was damaged. So they kept one person aboard as a sort of backup, wired in to everything that goes on – coordinating the engines, navigation, all weapons systems. – everything. It all channels through here, through me. As a backup.

So I'm the fail-safe. Locked in here, wired in for direct access. I'm never included in on anything to do with decisions: they filter and divert what comes to me all the time. 'We're letting you rest,' they say. 'Don't want your mind getting cluttered and stale.'

'Fear-filled and froze up, you mean?'

'If we need you in action, we want you fresh and alert and diving straight in. No need for knowledge other than your task.' I presume the principle is that if we've been all but wiped out, then I get in there and do the same thing to them. Then, like I said, there'll be nobody left. In theory, I know nothing about the overall situation, nor about the immediate local situation. If I'm let of the hooks, I'm autonomous, and I go do my job. That's the theory, anyway. In practice, I can log into my back-circuits down in my little module, and get a fair idea what's going on. Illicit Info Bypass, they'd call it if they knew.

This battle started some time ago – almost two days since the first attack commands came through. And three hours twenty-point-three-six since the last update. Lot of wondering between times, and since.

I know we've lost contact with two of our huge G-Size craft, and quite possibly several C-Size. They wouldn't even bother to register how many of us single-use ships have been lost – or *used*, as they phrase it. We're the smallest, A-Size; *suicide*, as they say.

'Yike!' Jolted. Hard.

I'm in instant Action Mode. *'Whoooooaah.'* Lurched. Bit sickening. I've mental-jabbed the *Go!*

Lurching again. Sliding away from the BG Master. My headset's live! I'm patched in! All-round action. *Shuggs! It's happening*. Calm. Soak in the situation – full-flood messaging filling me through – we've hit three of their Battleweights now. Complete destruction. *Shit – the lives lost – thousands*. Two of our biggies confirmed lost. Probably just as many dead on our side. Shit shit – don't bear thinking about – fifteen hundred on each. The only reason I'm suddenly linked in is that we're being sent in on a mission. Ha – mission? Death Run, more like. and we're going in.

I don't know if I want to spew up, piss myself, or do a long-lasting "Yesssssss" as I'm cut free and hurl off in a huge independent parabolic tangent.

And we really are set free. I'm following all the movement on the screens, mimicking it. I'm tapped in. *Shit!* It's not supposed to involve me actively. Just use my brain as a back-up facility without my awareness.

I'm live with it! It's going through me – I'm in the systems now. I log the navvy beams… locate the target. Full thrust on the instant. If we'd had peripheral crew, they'd be splushed and splattered by now – it always happened before. From the first second of the Off, I weave and twist, veer off… Seeking, seeking, searching the radar, vads, las-systems, infilyans… in blue light, UV, PD and vacuo beams. Pigalone knows where any enemy might be, I sure as Sh' hama have no idea and I'm twisting and spiralling, long long minins… eyes and seekers everywhere.

There!!!

Some massive reading on the screens. Pigalone knows what. Something enormous and hostile

Systems lock in automatically. It's targeted. But I have volitional control – me guiding, not auto-mack. I'm taking a different angle of approach… violent side-swerve. Barrel-rolling, spiralling in… No plan to it. No rules. No book. No prog. I do what I do.

It's looming fast. Massive great G or even H-Weight. Awesome. Ten thousand times the Valiant's size. The whole thing's like an ultra-modern building on Dighm, plus a complex tangle of massed antennae and weapons ports and pigalone knows what else. And he's gonna zap shit out of us – me – any sec now. I weave. Double-twist. I'm close in. I spin and whirl in random turns – like me and Valiant can do – they can't track us. Too fast. Nimble as fuck. Can't focus at this speed, especially so close.

A corner of my mind hopes it'll be instant – I'll be vapped. But I'm totally immersed in perathine semi-liquid in a para-electro-magnetic field. The strains of a hundred gee shouldn't get me – I'm gel-bathed by now – it was the time when previous crew members became smears on the walls. There's light beams and zap-bolts flashing through the vac. So close! Hard to tell how close – so fast I'm going – by the time a bolt's come through, I'm three turns down the aisle.

I'm in very close and fast. Too close for their guns and fields now… I hurtle round it, quarter speed, looking for a weak spot where a single bolt will zap the damn thing. That way, Valiant might stand a chance of surviving its total detonation. Fat chance – that thing goes up, I'm instant vapour.

God this thing is so vast.

There! I lock into a vortex-engine spot – where the power units are located. Lock in all weapons systems – open-blast and deep-penetration weapons. Set them all for go in a fraction… And fi—

Zeep bleep! Zeep. Zeep. Zeep. I never ever heard one before. Couldn't miss it now. Piercing.

It's surrendered!

There's no two ways about that. It had given in. Knew it was on the brink of being a disintegrating fire-mass. Must have lost too many others. My weapon systems froze up, then stood down when I jabbed acceptance. I could have rejected, and Valiant would have auto-fired. The Nemica ship would have gone up, and most likely us with it. *Single* Use, we are – me and Valiant. They emphasised that. I don't recall volunteering for this duty in the first place; I certainly wouldn't have done if they'd told us that before.

But – all interstellar rules said – Surrender means exactly that. They gave up. Shuggs – I was sweating down. Tension I didn't know I could get.

It kept up the zeep bleep… incessant. It meant it. It had to mean it. That bleep disables its own weapons systems. It would detonate them if any attempt was made to use them again.

All our big guys have it, too. Not us littlies, we're expendable, and there's no communication once we're turned loose. But the biggies – too much pointless loss of life when they brewed up – had to be a way to forestall total destruction – a last-second total surrender and self-disablement.

And this time – it had worked. Shuggs! It worked! They saved themselves with under one sec to spare.

Valiant was safe then. They couldn't attack; and I'd stood my weaponry down.

I slowed and peeled in behind it – as much as there is a "behind" – but in its blank spot, anyway. Just plain trusting that it couldn't fire anything. It should have totally disabled itself. It must have. It was Interstell Law.

My instructions? What the Triple F do I do next?

Thinking… thinking… My task now is to log back to Mother, keep them informed but not involved. I racked my internal memory-embed tracks for procedures on what to do now.

How deeply buried the instructions were. How simple – "Escort Surrendee to Base for Dee".

Which meant De-brief… De-commission… De-weaponise… De-bark officers… Whatever.

So basically, what was expected was that ESS Valiant – all ninety-eight vac-mass tonnes of her – would guide them back to our Forward Base… or perhaps Home Base. This struck me as being a mite risky if they'd found some way to override the zeep bleep and disable links. But, the Interstellar Monitors guaranteed it wasn't possible. I heard some of our teams had looked into by-passing the systems and scratched their balls. And I bet the opposition had been doing the same – scratching their egg sacs.

But. Orders is orders. So I'm expected to guide this NSC Volatility H-Weight right into Forward Base. Where, if they're better than the InterMons who set it up, they'll let loose with everything they've got. Starting with Valiant, I expect, to eliminate any possible pre-emption or retaliation. Maybe they're the same sort of suicide ship as us – not the same *kind*, same purpose. Maybe they're stripped down to minimum volunteer crew and packed with MT-85. That'd take half the solar system out, with the amount that thing could hold. Or at least the instant vaporisation of an average-sized moon. Or Forward Base.

I brain-fed what I knew to Mother. For information only. They had no say because the Topweight was in a close-down situation to prevent them being got at.

So here I am, float-strapped in here, basically with no choice, yet again. Rules said to guide them to Base. The zeep bleep gained me automatic control of their guidance system, and I slaved their engines to Valiant's.

Off we went. Me at left-centre-tail position. Nervous as a bag of quaker chicks on market day. And this uffing great monstrosity going first. Supposedly, this was so that Base could blast the bast, as the saying goes, if it looked like trying anything.

I had brief – minimal – contact with two of our other vessels – my own Mother Topweight, and some other that looped in. Almost entirely automatic systems. To keep them informed. I had to confirm a couple of keys so I could plan and set a course.

Set course, yes… For Forward Base. But, actually, the Regs said "Base", not specifically which one. There's a base back on Herith – Leisure Base. And the one on Spiro for ship repairs. So, "Base" is within my definition, not the ship's or the rules'. There's the Astro-tech Base between Gamma and Delta. That's forward. Forward enough, anyway. Or it was, a half-century back – storage and exchange now – usually unmanned these days.

So, if NSC Volatility has by-passed the safeties, and intends to eradicate our base… and Valiant with it. Hi ho – so be it – they'll get the wrong base.

The Brass did make it clear we're single-use, though. I don't think an A Class ever survived an actual outing before. Maybe I'll be a first. That'll bugger up their records.

Anyway, survive or not, I'm not too sure that I'm ever getting out of here. I'm not one hundred percent certain, but I think I'm either a wired-up brain in this module; or an ultra-connection to a living person's brain back at some Base somewhere. Be interesting to find out which, at the termination of this foray. Or not.

I'm kinda hoping it's the latter, and I can go on leave, have a few drinks, find a girl, maybe…

But I'm not holding my breath.

***

'He's the one.' Senior Guard Yoyi nodded along the bare metalwork, stark cages and cells of the space-side block. He's got to go. Soon.'

'Who'd he piss off?'

'Mas Sanggoft.'

'Sanggoft? The mining family?' Junior Guard Quish smiled in disbelief. 'Multi-trillionaire-type Sanggoft?'

'There's another Sanggoft?' He upped the glare filter against the blazing sun, and nodded out the windowport. 'That's all Sanggoft land down there.' The orbiting prison was enveloped in the freezing black shadow of the mostly-rock planet of Grýtt. Patches of lights were scattered across the surface, far below Khuk Penitentiary. 'Every light's a mine of one kind or another, and they're what provide most of this system's wealth; thanks almost entirely to Sanggoft Inc.'

'And we been ordered to get rid of this guy? How come?'

'Best not enquire, Quishy. We been *asked* to vack him; quietly. But I did hear he's in for Grand Theft SS. Tried to steal Sango's private space yacht – complete with his wife and kids.' Yoyi moved along the gantry and across to the main gangway.

'Kinda stupid. On his own?' Quishy pulled himself along the dully-shining panels and all-direction ladders.

'Five of'em.' SG Yoyi steadied himself expertly on the end of the gantry and paused. 'He was the pilot. And now, he's the only survivor; just the last in the accident queue since they were caught. And his time's up.'

They pulled along three-dozen more cell spaces. 'Yo! 296!'

The figure at the next cell stood erect and identified himself, 'Sir. XV8296. Prisoner Keizur, S. Present, Sir.'

'Duty task for you, 296. Now. JG Quish will escort you to the dock for suiting up. You got a spell outside.'

***

At least it took me out the cage for a shift, and into the vack. The suits are all ill-fitting and probably leaky, but it's prison issue, so it's what you get. Air don't seem too pure in'em, either – most likely harbouring a complete menagerie of bugs and fungi. 'Yeah, well, if it don't kill me, it'll immune me against another set of microbes.'

'It's another welding job in the Terminal Space,' the Maintenance Off-C told me.

'You got a half-day shift in there, 296.' That bastard Quish might be new, but he knew how to smirk, alright.

'Oxy's filled. Heat and jet power fully charged. Pick you own line and locking point and get outside. Start on Panel 98 and work your way along.'

'You know the routine.'

Yeah, I did – it was repairing panels inside the entrance and exit tube for the whole station. This's more'n just the penal facility; it's the transfer hub for ships collecting and discharging people and goods heading for other systems, as well as being the terminus for this planet. Huh, Grýtt indeed.

That tunnel is vast. It's intimidating. You're inside a space that's big enough to accommodate any ship, including the passenger cruisers and mining bulk carriers. And there's at least a dozen big vessels every day, heading to and from light-years-away systems, plus plenty of small local craft use the place. When a biggy's due in, the tunnel lights up in a mass of coloured panels that show the force-field's on and powering up. It'll suck any craft in and hold it while it's directed to a berth off to one side for disembarking. Then the reverse when one's set to depart.

It is awesome to be in there. So huge, like having your own multi-coloured sky lit up all around you. Scary-nervy, too. You duck for cover when the lights power up, or you get powered-up and ejected yourself.

The small local traffic don't need the whole terminal to light-up – they just zip in and out when they like, dodging the cruisers and mining freighters, like I used to do myself, over on Stray. But that was before I let myself get suckered into some stupid scheme to steal a smart, ultra-fast yacht. I wanted to release the passengers at the first opp; but the others were fixed on ransoming them, or raping them if the money didn't come through. And we were stupid enough to stay in one place bickering about it.

When you're suited up in the Terminal Space, it's hard work, whatever you're doing. Prison suits were made for security, not comfort or safety, and my job on this shift was to re-weld a series of panel frames back in place. It involved floating from one to another, secured on a long line, and using a small hand-jet for propulsion. That was easy like I'm accustomed to, but the work itself is strenuous and awkward, positioning high-mass girders into place, and spot-welding them down. And there they stay, till the next reckless jockey gives them a clout with his back-end.

It passes the time, and I'm not locked in a ten-by-ten, at least – *Damn! Half-way into my shift, and I'm practically out of prop power already – s'okay, I can hand-haul back in if the jet-pack gives up.*

Ay-yih... The panel I was working on – the size of a cabin roof – was starting to glow. 'Something big's coming in or leaving. I shouldn't be out here in traffic.' All around, the panels were lighting up, a spectrum of colours lining the whole cavernous tunnel. Super-impressive on the inside, but I best not be on the up-side, so I reel towards the nearest bolt-hole space where I can duck in for a twenty-min breather.

'Uffff!' Hit from behind. Hard. And I'm spinning, tumbling down the tunnel, past the huge glowing panels towards the empty stuff outside. Saw a small mixed-freight cargoer heading out. *Careless bastard. Caught me. Rushing to get out before whatever giant's expected in or out. Be alright, pull myself in...* 'Damn… line's snapped.'

About a ship's length of line trailed behind me. 'Shyke – this's serious.' I even said it aloud. After a dozen minins rolling over and over, and finding the hand-jet was out of power, and the communi-rad was dead, I knew I was just as dead. And inside, I'm panicking and gibbering, 'Not like this… not like this…'

Couple of hours, the universe spinning around me as I roll away. Hard to see much that makes sense when you're spinning, but I got the impression I was heading into the derelicts' parking orbit. *Just maybe there'll be something to hook onto.*

I bounced into one huge, slightly rounded hull without even seeing it in advance – me spinning, and the hulk black against black. I tried the magnetics, but I'd already bounced too far. Wouldn't have helped, anyway. Who's gonna find me out here?

I'm not going to open the valve – that'd be suicide, and Gov would get its hands on my gear. Like it's worth more'n two creds? If I die natural, it's their fault, and my celly, Ikey, would have my bits – clothes and stuff. We got an agreement.

Anyway, I stopped scrabbling at the vack. Nothing I can do out here. Total black. Sun-outlined edges of silver floating silently past, spinning still. A few other wrecks, abandoned, some being stripped. Me spinning, not them. Whole planet's rolling right round me three or four times a minin. Damn typical of me – end my days drifting through a junk orbit.

I expect I'd see a few star points if only they'd keep still… tried the power jet again – just a fraction left this time. Slowed my spin slightly. Not enough to guide me any direction. Where's to go?

T'ain't right, going like this… Yeah? How'd you want to go? Least it don't hurt. Yet. Getting woozy. Side-swiped by some Vanguard class in the Terminal Tunnel. *Thoughtless is all. Not looking. Rushing. Done it myself. Never hit anybody, though. Few dents.* Never even saw whatever the panels lit up for. If anything. Maybe just testing.

I talk to myself a lot – you do when you're on a solo piloting trip somewhere, or in a cell, or a suit bound for nowhere. *Can't blame the guy… No? I blame him – I never did that.* Air'll be gone soon, foul already. Stinks in here. Getting cold, too. Feet's gone. Fingers, too. Getting chokey in my head. Too much oxy recycling. *Take the needle. Get it over. Can't do that – I'd never face myself again…* I know I'm rambling. Don't care. Won't face anybody again. My Maker, maybe – she's got things to answer for. *She'll not want to see you. Won't give her no choice if I'm dead.* S'all fading, so cold. Black. On my own – how it's always been…

***

'It's a guy. He's dead. Nano-froze and de-oxy'd. Bunch of kids brought it in, partying out in the junk park. It's a Penitentiary suit – prisoner on out-work duty. They mention anybody missing?' Merinya heaved the rigid body up, its cumbersome suit catching on the side rail of the gurn. 'They're not heavy in near-zero G, but they're awkward, just the same. Got a name for him?

'Yeah, prison reported one gone a couple of wekks ago. Line snapped while out, repairing the buffer-plates in the in-out runnel. Number and name – Prisoner XV8296. Keizur S.'

'Down in Terminal Space, huh? They don't call it that for no reason – the number lost in there. More'n a dozen this year already – I reckon they're trying to thin their overpopulation out. Had a couple with severed lines; one with nitro instead of oxy in the back-up tank.'

'Yeah, if it ain't the warp effect short-circuiting or pre-warming, then it'll be some jockey pilot coming or going out too cundering fast – they know the magnos'll stop'em actually hitting anything solid.'

The two mortuary staff rolled the body over, peering into the visor. 'Trouble is, people aren't all that solid.'

They looked at the corpse before them. 'He's lucky: they found him magnet-stuck on the engine cowling of a tanker that some crew's working on. I suspect they weren't just partying – seeing what was thievable, too.'

'Wasn't all that lucky – he's still dead.'

'Name of Keizur? Where's a name like that come from? Mustn't have been a good boy if he was in the jail.' Coggsy glanced through the keypad data, looked into the newly-exposed face as the visor plate came away. ‘Keizur… Steg Keizur.’

‘Another off-worlder getting himself into bother.’ Merinya gazed at the frozen pallid face. ‘Fixing the buffer plates, was he? Always somebody getting tapped by one careless cargo-dongo or another.’

‘They’ll split their own skin wide one of these days.’

‘They won’t do it again if they do. You already done the padwork? Registered the death?’

‘Yeah – Prison don’t wanna know. They’re on a budget. Looks bad on their books. Up to us to dispose of him now.

’Like we’re not on a budget?’

‘Maybe you shouldn’a registered him so quick – we could’a pushed him back out for free. Not now he’s registered, though; we ain’t allowed to litter.’

‘We can just dump him into burn-up orbit with the next batch who actually want to end up as a fiery trail

‘Kay; just get him out the suit. If Pen don’t want the body, they ain’t getting the suit back, either – it’ll fetch a few creds on sBay. Help defray the disposal cost.’

‘Could let him de-frog and slip him in the garbage mincer on off-time?’

‘Come on, Coggsy – I ain't doing that again – there was an eyeball turned up in somebody’s dinner once before. Just leave him here to de-frog. I’ll check on space in the chavel-grinder out at that new construction they’re doing. That’ll be cheaper, less fuss. No risk of comebacks.’

***

‘Coggsy? You bring this corpse in last night’

'Reene? That you? Yeah, me and Merinya. What about it?'

'It's above room temp. I stuck a link on it, and there's a glimmer of life. Just got a very slow flutter-pulse – ahh, another. Prison's using old-style see-me-off in the suit, by the smell of it. Maybe think it's kinder—'

'The Pen? Kind? Just the opposite; probably to spin it out for them. Guards hate the Crims. It'll likely to have been deliberate – bad air, narco him, something like that. Festering fungus in there, too?'

'Whatever, he ain't dead. Not quite. And before you ask, No. I'm not going to finish the job.' She sniffed suspiciously around the naked near-corpse.

'He *is* dead. I registered him dead, so legally he must be. He has to be. Law says so.'

'You go tell him, then.'

Coggsy looked at the erstwhile body. Looked healthy – for a corpse and prisoner. 'Maybe there's an alternative. Let's give him time to wake; see if he's got all his brain cells intact and joined-up.'

***

They helped me out the big bare mortuary room with all the white and satin steel, into a side room with seats and a grey, old-blood-spattered gown to pull round myself. Tall feller and a woman. Couldn't believe I was still alive – how the fryke?

'No idea. Some youngsters found you stuck on a wreck, brought you in. Dosed up with fungus, pills, narco, nano-freeze… probably every disease that anybody who ever wore that suit was carrying.'

'Anyway,' the woman started up, 'You're not out the vack yet. This is kinda awkward…'

‘What? You just send me back and they have another go next wekk.’

‘They don’t want you back – you’re off their screens now.’

‘And officially, you’re off ours, too – we registered your death two days ago.’

This was sounding ominous. ‘You gonna airlock me? The meat grinder? Do I get stuck in a firing tube?’

‘We have considered those options, yes.’ The guy didn’t even look embarrassed when he admitted it. ‘But perhaps there’s a way out of this that doesn’t involve any expense or awkward Qs.’

‘Oh?’ This really didn’t sound good. ‘Hmm?’ I don’t think I felt up to making a dash for the door, especially not laid-out bollock-bare on a flatable.

‘Suppose you wanna be someone else? You ever did?’

‘Sure, anybody sep a lifer.’

‘Kay – we got a heap of presumed-deadies—'

‘Presumed?’ Yet more of an ominous feel to it.

‘People who vanished with no other explanation and no body. Like you, spun off planetwards, burned-up, crushed to nothing, still attached to a ship that went vac-wards… explosion… working inside a drive unit when they tested it… you know the sort of thing. Happens all the time.’

‘Yeah, tell me about it.’ I heard tales like that every day for the last two years.

‘What we have here is you – a non-body who’s registered dead. There’s nothing we can do – the padwork’s more final than you are – gone off. All official.

'However,' the guy was getting to the point now. I hoped. 'If it's a *presumed* dead – then we keep the padwork in case they turn up. Nothing finalised.'

'Never have done yet.'

'But if they did, we have the docs ready—'

'And they'd be able to carry on where they, er, left off.'

They were looking damned crafty here, pair of them.

'You, in fact, are the first of our Presumeds to resurface.'

'I am? Which one am I?' This was taking some understanding, the state my head was in.'

A look of muted triumph, the tall attendant dropped a loose pack of ID docs onto the low table. 'Which one do you want to be?'

'These are the last ten or a dozen presumies. Have a look through them. Any of them could be found alive – *like here and now – he gave me the hard meaningful look.* So take your time – look through. Decide who you are.'

'There's more in the cabinets, but you don't want to be going back too far. Affairs are settled, folk've moved on. Forgotten you…'

'You might get away with being a woman, if you fancy a change?

'Give us a shout if you want any help. Another hot drink? Ryke stew? Smoke?'

I nodded. 'All of'em, with my gratitude.' *This is completely beyond. I'm dead. I know I am. I was out there in the vack. Pushed out the Terminal Space. No way back from that.*

Hardly even beginning to recover, I started to flip through the little scatter of docs. Couple of them were rich; well-off, anyway. Maybe beaten by the pressure of work? Bumped off? Kidnapped? Two were long-partnered – one a woman – too many complications. I think my partner would notice the difference. One from Exig – who speaks that? Moderately comfortable, was on a tour-trip of the Perdian Cluster sights… Another guy looked dodgy – Fed notice in the docs – wanted for something technical and serious. I'd end up back in PD. One's a Fingers – got the extra-long bones? Don't think I'd have much credibility with that ID.

My head was still dull and swirling a bit. Not really believing any of this was happening – had to be some dream. I'm still out there. But they seem gen. And I'm looking through these docs and plaspaps. Couple of them got pics – one guy's ugly. *No wonder he vanished…*

The woman's a looker. Yeah, be nice to be in her boots – or maybe not her boots, exactly.

A youngish man with enough cash to buy his own cargoer – *Yeah, Right, and all the trouble and strings that'd go with it.*

How bout this one? Colourful name – Blue. S'all it says about him. No pic. No birth planet. No first name. A few creds to the name – couple of hundred. *Not exactly rich, huh?*

My two morto friends popped back in with the snack and smokes. 'How's it going? Need anything?'

'I'm wondering about this one…'

They skipped into the keypad and docs. 'Probably an itinerant, just called himself Blue. It's a nickname – often used as a cover in some places.'

'Just means he didn't want a real name sticking on him.'

'Yeah, we had a few like that, inside.' *Like the guys in the cages either side of mine.*

'Most likely just passing through – doing a few jobs to stay breathing. Something screwed him up.'

'You thinking of being him?'

'Maybe. Might be safest. Least known, least to crop up later.'

'Yeah – why not?' Reene liked the idea. 'Hell, feller, you could easily become him – give yourself a first name. Make his nickname your official name.'

'What? Blue? As my new real name?'

'Sure, why not? It's as good as anything.'

They were both thinking about it, 'Off to a fresh start.'

'New horizons for you…'

'Stick with Blue – that's what's on the paperwork; and keep some of your own name, in case you say it sometimes, not thinking.'

I thought about that, 'Yeah, why not, if I adapt my real name. Maybe Steg Blue? Keizur Blue?'

'Keizur S Blue?'

'No. You want something more positive. You'll be free…'

'You'll have a few creds. No history…'

'Fresh ships and planets new…'

'Whole new start for you...'

'How about Skeizur Blue?'

THE BOMB MAN

'It's you, isn't it?'

The voice made me jump. *I find a diner with a starview at the Zenec Orbital Terminal, and somebody's still going to come for a chat.* Reluctantly raising my eyes from my e-dried battered gunfish and beaker of poli-tar, I saw this skinny woman in off-duty uniform. 'No. I'm not me,' I told her, and picked the drink up. *Hmm, I know you from somewhere.*

'You remember Kerith?'

The worst possible beginning to anything. *I know you... It'll come to me. Not now, go away. Not relive that time. Kerith. Not ever.*

'It was you. At Kerith.' Big smile, she wasn't going.

'You're not asking *if* I remember, you must know I was. You're here to screw me up?'

Nobody's forgotten. My name is known. The name I had then. They shouldn't know. In theory, it was an ultra-guarded secret. Guaranteed anonymity. Even on the ship, no-one would know. Somebody leaked me the same day. Accompanied by a single Vid-pic of me actually doing it.

'You were the bomb man on the Mother of God.' She stood there in front of me. Brazen. Saying it aloud. Just like that. In front of other people in the lounge.

The Bomb Man. 'You think I need to be told who I was? Who I still am? You're a fool.' *I know you. There's something more terrible going on here.*

Yes, that day. The day we annihilated Kerith. Or, as I used to be told most every day, 'It wasn't *we*. It was *you* personally who obliterated that whole planet. Brought about a terrible death for six billion people. The Keriths, who were fellow sentient beings...' *Yes, I know, by far the greatest catastrophe in civilised history. Six billion deaths. Carried out by me. Wilfully.*

All that time ago... Decades back. Do I remember it? After all this time? 'Go away,' I told her. 'Leave me alone. Just… Leave me be.'

**

She's looking soft-serious, still standing before me, her mere presence ruining my already meagrous meal as if with too much sour-salt. *You practise that look, hmm? I do recall. Yes, I know you. No. I don't actually know you. I've seen you before, that's all. Once.*

'It was a long time ago. Do you remember?'

I gave up, sighed and put my drink down. 'Seventy-nine years, three dodecs and two days, Uni-Time? Seventy-six years seven deccs in Terrath Time. One hundred eighty… Yes, I remember Kerith. Sometimes. Now and again.'

Do I remember when it was my name picked out the cayat? There had been an announcement that someone aboard would be randomly chosen "to perform the object task of our expedition." The whole point of Destroyer-Class Ultima Space vessels was to engage the enemy in "an Ultimate Manner". In the engines unit, we never had any idea where we were, or who the enemy might be, much less what we were actually doing, other than keeping the time-drives in phase. Do I recall when an officer came for me, down in the engine depths of the Mother of God? And said, 'It's you who was picked.' How my stomach fell. My heart stopped. And I didn't breathe? Yes, I remember.

Standing there. In the Operations Command room, on some level that was scarcely a rumour down in Engines. When the announcement was made, I didn't dream it could even be anyone I knew. Far less consider the chances of it being me. But it was. *Why me out of more than a thousand officers, crew and troopers aboard that ship?*

I had to do it. There was no choice. *It's not like I bare-handedly strangled them all. All six billion.*

I pressed a button. Large. Red. With a guard over it. It had to be unlocked by two senior officers. Why didn't *they* push the button? Two others certified it. They stepped back. I was motioned forward. *You ask if I remember?*

A million pixels per nano-second I remember. I breathed twice, deeply. Glanced sideways at some woman officer on my left. She looked more nervous than me. She wore a low-peak cap with silver braid – Special Force. Never seen one before. But I wouldn't have done, would I? Me being Third Crew in Drive Maintenance? There's nobody below me. I never even meet our own officers, much less Special Force visiting High-ups.

Commodore Hadyn was there, too. I'd seen him on the T-vids. Looked older in the Command Room. He was avoiding eye contact with me. *I'm too low for you, huh?* All the others must have felt the same.

I wasn't nervous. I was cold and dead inside. I flexed my lips once. Swallowed once. It was three steps forward. I took them. One at a time. I reached. Put my right forefinger on the button. Glanced at the Special

Forces woman in low-peak silver braid. Looked the other direction at Commodore Hadyn. Very pale blue eyes, just for a fractioned second. An almost imperceptible nod. I pressed.

I waited. They looked at screens. At data streams. Nodded to each other. 'This way,' someone said. And I was walking out with a double escort, back to the Drive unit.

'What now?' I asked, back in the familiar pale green light and oily static aroma.

'Whatever your duties entail.' The two escort troopers stepped away from me. It was over.

It was over for them, for the High Commanders, and, I learned later, it was over for the Keriths within the hour. All *six* billion. Exactly how, I didn't know. Not at the time.

**

The queue for Number 8 Airlock was beginning to form. That's mine – the ship to Falkan for my next contract. I'll need to go soon. I lifted my drink again. *I do know you. Aged almost eighty years. What's that, these days? Half a lifetime.* 'Why are you here?' I asked her

'To see you.'

I drank. *If you're going to be stupid – nobody comes or goes anywhere to see me.* 'I do recognise you.'

'After seventy-nine years?'

'You're not in your silver-braid uniform now. You've moved on.'

'You haven't.' Her eyes dotted over me. Disparaging my appearance. 'You took some finding.'

'Not enough, clearly.' I must vanish once more. I wasn't going to ask why again. *You have until my drink is drained. Then I'll be gone. I have contingencies. I shall not be found by anyone else. People coming and speaking to me in order to screw me up in some way. This I do not need. Two more swallows and I shall forever vanish from your sight. The gunfish can deep-fry themselves. Maybe on Sigmund they won't have such cheap and unappealing garbage to eat?*

One swallow left. Get round to it, woman.

Abruptly, she sat.

'I was the Officer in Command of the whole expedition. It was my task to initiate the event… to press the button.'

'But?' I knew, stomach-sinkingly, what she was going to say.

'It should have been the day before. I had spent so much time planning, and discussing the alternative, and the effects and ramifications, I was too deep in it. I couldn't do it.'

'You had a Command Room full of button-pushers.'

'They all refused, "It's your responsibility," they insisted. I had the idea to hold the random, anonymised, no-blame lottery. Commodore Hadyn agreed; the need was pressing by then.'

Waiting for my reaction is eighty years too late, lady. Nothing makes any different now. It'll not chase six billion ghosts away from my shoulders.

'I… I built my career after that, went on to much higher things. I'm Supreme Commander Special Force now – for the whole Federation.'

'I know what Supreme means.'

She was silent, wanting more from me. I provided it, 'And the Vid-pic of me doing it? Was that you, too.'

She coloured up.

'To prove it wasn't you? So family and friends wouldn't think you were such a callous mass-annihilator? Should it ever be necessary, or convenient, to deny it?'

Her eyes dropped.

Yes... there's more. I waited. *But you're back in Indecision Mood, aren't you? Like you were that day? I can wait. Come on, Supreme Being Stand-in, there's more. Tell me. You think I don't know?*

The undisclosed guilt was still there, all over her. *I bet you never shuffled so uncomfortably before, did you? Come on... Volunteer it. Don't make me prompt you.*

'I... I knew the rumour would instantly finger-point at me. And once in the sights, never completely out of them. So I pre-empted the release of information, with that picture.'

I knew that already: I'd worked it out within a day of being fingered. So obvious. 'And now, what do you seek from me? Not forgiveness. That's for the ghosts of Kerith to dispense or withhold.'

An eye flicker and waved finger elicited two fresh drinks from a roving server. She took one, sipped. Then drained it. *Yes. There is more. You need to tell me everything. You'll not escape your own guilt until you do. And nor will I. So... come on. Say it.*

Starzabove! It must weigh heavy. Tell me. I already know.

'I... I...' She faltered. Reached for my drink.

I stopped her hand. 'Tell me first. It's only the two of us. We should be honest with ourselves, if no-one else.'

'It... It wasn't random. I picked you when I looked through the Mother of God's crew manifest. You looked like someone to inculpate. The sort of face everyone could easily blame. Regular and nondescript.'

There. That's it. She'd let go of herself. I let go of her. She raised the beaker, and lowered it without drinking. 'I'm glad you know.' She heaved in a deep sigh.

Taking my drink from her, I sipped, and passed it back. 'I've known since the day.' *When you think about little else, you speculate, suspect and theorise very quickly.*

In silence, we shared the drink.

'I think,' I eventually said, 'this is no longer a burden carried separately, nor even a burden shared. It's a burden lifted. I feel my weight of Kerith ghosts fading.'

'Are they all coming to me?' Her eyes asked as much as her lips.

'No. They're fading. We only needed to share. We'll be better now.' I managed a smile, 'I have a ship to catch.'

***

THE DISPUTED PLANET OF ALGA THOR

This moment for me, the heliotrope.
To which I turn in pride and hope
For peace between us and the Androlope.
My life to here's been a kaleidoscope
Of dreams; I burst with joy, can barely cope

With this momentous day.
For peace between us, this we pray.
I carry the flag and lead the play.
On wheels of silver I slowly sway
To the musical lilt of night and day.

To the summit I'm borne
With faith that peace is here reborn;
That strife of old be erased at dawn.
All my People's prayers I've borne
To embody them I'm ever sworn.

---oOo---

She carried our future, Melon-ya Xing
Rare she was, as a rainbow ring.
Treasured by all as a butterfly's wing.
In the early blush of a Sylvan spring
She died a charred and screaming *thing*.

In a blaze of fire, they burned her there,
Roasted alive in the midst of prayer.

My daughter. Oh, my daughter fair.
In raging fury we took revenge and none did spare;
We butchered them all, like zax in the lair.

This the report of our Council of War
On the riddance of all that we abhor,
To end the conflict born of yore.
The Androlope filth to be seen no more
On the precious planet of Alga Thor.

---oOo---

Darratt Empire, High Command.
Enquiries done. Our verdicts stand.
The cursed People we reprimand
We find *them* guilty: this *they* planned,
To fault the Androlope out of hand.

They it was who murdered their own;
Burned her down, her life not grown.
To blame their foe and claim the throne
Of Alga Thor for themselves alone.
It's established now: the evidence known.

This Empire judgement, now declared:
To let the People stay we're not prepared.
They are banned from Alga Thor; their evil bared.
To break the Peace, it was they who dared.
This planet with *them* shall never be shared.

------oOo------

THE NEW COLONISTS

'Come on, Ladies,' Supervisor Lagg told us, 'you got another ten minutes, then you gotta choose which one.'

'It's a big decision, Super,' Bella said. 'I bet you had more time to decide yourself.'

I wasn't going to argue, I'm just grateful to be here. But, now I am here, I want to be sure I pick right. 'Just give me a minin, huh, Super?' Lords below, my aching bones, I didn't want to spin this out any longer than necessary, but it really would be worthwhile taking as long as I needed.

Lagg grumped, but he nodded and backed off, so we carried on peering through the one-way glass at the dozen or so newcomers loafing around in the reception lounge. I wasn't especially impressed with any of them. 'Not a great bunch to pick from, are they? Bit disappointing, really – there's not one who actually appeals.'

'I'm looking at the tall woman with boobs like the tyres on my swamp tractor,' Bella said. 'Talk about leading the way. Either her or the rounded one; she's a good bit younger, too. But if none of them suits *you*, Donna, broaden your view. There's nothing to stop you considering one of the men. That'd make a change.'

‘They *are* your only choice, Ladies.’ Lagg butted in, ‘Maybe they aren’t as great as some others in the past, but it could be years before the next batch is brought here. So sure, look over the men. Just get a move on, eh?’

I considered my aching back, as well as the men. They hadn’t occurred to me as an option, so I regarded the assembly with new eyes, ‘Never know, one of them might appeal, I suppose.’ My legs were shaking a bit with the ague, too. I’d need to sit down before too long.

It took one minute to appraise them. ‘Well, there’s only a couple who are in the young and fit category. I suppose *he* looks alright.’

Bella was more than a mite dubious about my narrowing-down. ‘Who? The shave-head with the tattoos? Y’ not serious?’

‘It was your idea to look at the men. He’s young. Big. Has good muscles. And I’ve spent more than long enough looking at all the others. I’m getting cholled off with this.’

‘We don’t get to choose who comes here,’ as if Lagg needed to remind us. ‘Only what happens when they arrive. Fylaki’s a prison planet, remember, so make the most of them, Ladies; new settlements are being opened up all over this planet and the other two penal worlds. So the groups that are sent to us aren’t as big, or as frequent, as they once were.’

We looked again. 'How about that smaller one? Bristly blond hair and chisel-chin,' Bella suggested.

'He was my other possibility, but he's littler than I am. If I'm having a man, he's not going to be the size of spanner.'

It took me another two minutes to finally decide. Given the choice offered, I accepted I was in for a complete change this time, and focused on Ink-head with muscles and attitude. But Bella, of course, still couldn't decide between Inflate-a-chest and the plump one who was fifteen years younger.

'I'll bring Tattoos and your twosome into the side-lounge,' Lagg offered, checking his pad. 'His name's Gonnor. He's from a planet called Revelle. They've been having a clampdown on violent crime of late. A one-man terroriser-cum-home invader, he is. I'll chat with them while you watch – remember you're not allowed to meet them in person beforehand; and don't forget we haven't got all day – and there's others waiting to make their pick.'

We saw him approach our three convict-colonists as they were helping themselves to more of the freebie drinks. And we watched and listened while they all chatted about their hopes and expectations for their time here on Fylaki.

'Hard labour sure don't appeal.' And this from Ink-head – the original muscle-guy, grinning round a new environment to victimise.

'I just want out of this awful marshalling centre.'

'If I must work, then something cusho, indoors, where I don't get supervised too closely. I'll look round and see where there are opportunities.'

'No, I got no specific skills,' Inky took pride in bragging. 'Don't need no more than I already got.'

'It was here or execution.' Boobs shrugged, smirking, 'for what I did to those two men.'

'As long as you feed me…' the all-over-rounded option was saying, 'I don't really mind. I'm not very good at anything, though.'

'A short diet'd soon sort her out. You'd be alright with her,' I encouraged Bella, but she was *still* undecided, and I was getting impatient with her, so I bleeped down and gave Lagg the TTO for mine. A second later, he's giving me and Ink-head the nod. Plus a little extra something in Inky's drinky.

'Ah,' he was suddenly saying, as though he'd just received an unexpected earpiece message, 'it's just coming through. We've found you a placement with an experienced colonist, a former convict herself. You want to come along with me? And we'll introduce you shortly? Ohh, feeling a touch tired, are you, Gonnor? Well, you can rest up through here for a while – there's a very comfortable couch.'

I went along to the Meet and Greet room that was allocated to me, adjacent to the one that my be-muscled friend-to-be was settling into. Ten minutes later, Lagg had Ink-head settled and wired up, and had come through to fit me up to the transfer apparatus.

'Yes, Prisoner Gonnor's insentient already – the trichloro works fast. You might have a hangover when you come round, though – he's been drinking solidly since arrival.' He checked all my NC electrodes one last time, went to the wall console and studied the readings for long moments, eventually concluding, 'Fine, the system's working perfectly. Good balance. One last chance to change your mind, Donna? No? Fine. Hand-print here, then.'

Settling back, I was immersed virtually instantly, my mind blanking as though falling asleep. Images hurtling through… a veritable high-speed blur of sounds. Nose tickling with a trillion unidentified aromas…

It was a slow process – several hours, but it couldn't be rushed or interrupted – the facility was still embarrassed about the one-and-only time the transfer had gone wrong, and Josie M'ween and some huge hairy man called Keet had each woken up as a mental mixture of themselves and each other. She's now called Josie M'bign, he's Para Keet, and no-one has any idea what to do with them next.

It's all so carefully done now, with endless checks and backups, and both parties sealed in for the duration. Very contented with my suddenly-expanded future, I let the tronix take me over… *I'll wake up in the other room later, with my new body. It'll be a relief to be out of this decrepit old carcass…*

Sitting up… slightly dizzy. Looking around, *Yes! I'm in a man's body.* And… considering… these tattoos could grow on me, I suppose – some are quite artistic, in a brutish sort of way.

I feel down… Wow! I am! A man! To be on the inside, as it were. *Mmm, feels gooood.* I know a few of my friends who'll go for a body like this. Oops – perhaps I shouldn't be lingering quite so long on first exploration of my new self…

This replacement system helps to solve the integration problem with new arrivals, though it was far worse in the old days when large groups of unreformed criminals were simply dumped here. That's how it was when I arrived – member of a Girl-Gang that was scoured out and deported en masse from Nucida. But I learned, behaved, worked, settled and survived for years, developing a lot of engineering skills and experience over the decades.

But I was attacked and chewed up by a pack of predfangs when we were out on Dryland Agri-district fixing an irrigation station one time. Would have been fatal, especially at my advanced age then, but I came round in a different body, a new-arrival woman who'd been stealing again, and had violently attacked the officers who caught her.

Before that, I had no idea that body-mind exchange was possible. 'Your senior wardens in Engineering must consider you a valuable prisoner-worker, Donna,' the transfer supervisor told me. 'So it makes sense to swap you into a body that can keep giving useful service to the Department.'

'It's not totally new technology,' one of the other officers said. 'But we certainly don't want it to become common knowledge. We'll monitor you; the new you is young and healthy. The previous occupant was utterly immune to reform, so she's been moved into your torn-up frame, where she won't be any further trouble – she'll die of the predfangs' wounds within the day.'

I had nearly sixty years in her rather fine body. Good years, rising in the prisoner ranks, probation, full-trusted status and semi-independence. But when the opportunity arose, I was happy to ditch her creaking joints for the most recent set, and continue my unexpectedly-prolonged and satisfying life.

This past year or so, that body had been coming to its end-time, and – My Thanks to the Gods – I was invited to choose a new body, so I must still be valued. Not a great choice when the high officers have picked through them, but – and it's very important – these offerings are considerably younger and fitter than my previous body, and are guaranteed disease-free.

'It was such a waste of time and money in the early days,' Lagg told me on my last exchange, 'trying to rehabilitate some of them, or force them to work. Then their start-up allocation fund ran out, and we'd dump them out in the far wilds. We were squandering money, and robust young bodies that could be more gainfully used by experienced, productive and well-adjusted minds, such as yours. Why would we want to lose someone like you, when we can swap you over soon after their arrival? It saves time and effort, as well as diverting the start-up fund into more promising projects.

'There's now almost no wastage of skills and knowledge on Fylaki. We have the best efficiency rating in the Tri-planet Penal consortium.'

So, with another longer-life opportunity like this, what else might I do? I'll see how I get along with being in a man's body – feels strong… good musculature. And all these tattoos are certainly different. Must let my hair grow, cover them up. Maybe I'll tackle some of the heavier works projects on the outside; the more physically challenging jobs for a change. I'll need a bigger bed and chairs at home. I'll find out what sex is really like for men— Piglo! I hope he's not an SL!

Newly-aged and gender-re-assigned, Gonnor should find it interesting, being an elderly, arthritic woman. Until she's sent out to some frontier fringe camp to test the perimeter security, and finds herself up against a pack of cunning and aggressive predfangs. See if she's got the quick wits, speed and strength to outrun them. I know I never could.

I wonder which one Bella finally chose. The one with the boobs looked over-used already, but she'd sure attract all the attention Bella usually craves. Or she'd look good in plump. She'll introduce herself sometime, I expect. And I'll re-introduce her to the new me – I can't stay as Donna.

I think I'll call myself Goner.

***

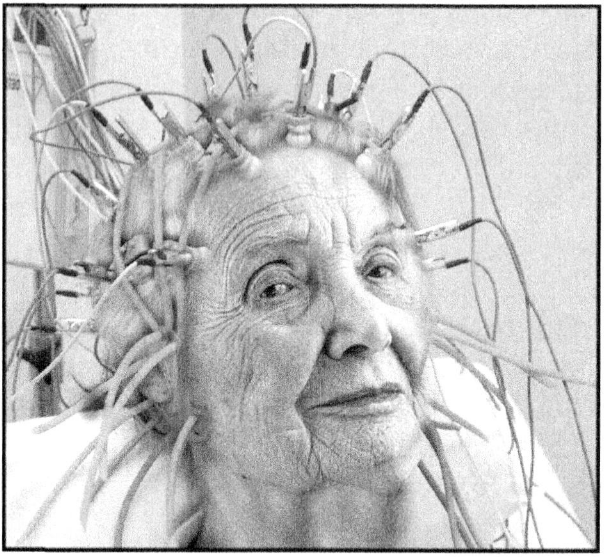

THE NEW REALITY

I fell for it! I'm the smartest-looking and thinking girl in Cygnus Sector, and I never even saw it coming. Not till I was out of it, and bitch-ditched here without anything. Totally without. Except clothes? I still had clothes. I should never be here – or the other places – in the first place, second place or any other place.

If I ever see Smiley-with-a-StunGun again, he's going to have so much time to regret this. I been conned by some thieving turdrag. He stole my spaceship! Koi – so it isn't exactly *my* ship – but I'm responsible for it. I'm the rep at the sales station and I do the rentals and purchasing sales. I take clients out on trial runs – using my judgement on their seriousness of likely buying.

I'm only doing the turdy job because I'm already on punishment probation for a year. The punishment being getting dumped on Flentice as a mechanic and salesbod in a spaceyard, rentals and salesroom. Not the biggies – freighters and suchlike; more the personals, family jigs, sporties, stripped-off ex-military ships and the like. So, of course, I know all the craft inside out because I've worked on them, fixed them, polished them up. I guarantee their vac-worthiness – C-guy gives me a lot of responsibility. 'Too much,' he's going to say after this. And then I'm deep deep deep in dung-dung-dung. While I'm already on punishment P.

Oh shigh! I should have been double-promoted for what I did on Magnus, not dumped on Flentice and out-conned by some scumbag who wants a test run, "I'll need to give the Red Spirit Racer a decent run if I'm going to hire her for a year,' he says, all smiles and sincere. And I believed him and his fake credit transfer. And the bastard pulls out a stunner and big smile. Right between my eyes. Saw the flash – UV indigo. Big fading smile.

***

So now I'm coming round in a ditch, edge of a backvac spaceport somewhere. Literally ditched. Things are not going well with my life of late. 'Just because I was part of the Fed Space Force that went a fraction overboard in chastising and pacifying a rebel group on Magnus.' I told'em at The Enquiry, 'I was following orders. To the letter and dot.' I'm not privy to the punishments meted out to the FS officers who'd done the ordering, but, as a full Flag Sergeant leading the advance attack, the high command expected me to have questioned, refused, re-checked, reported – deserted, even – rather than follow orders from Above.

'All of which offences are punishable by death,' I pointed out to'em.

And the headshed officers sitting round, chewing the cymbo mints, doing the questioning said, 'Yes, you should have taken that way out.' Pack of embroidered Fracktoes. If I ever find one on a dark night, back of a bar, or in the hold of some leaky tub… They'll know. I bet my kill-skill rating is ten times higher than theirs – any three of them put together.

Justice, huh? For doing my ordered duty, I copped more time "on parade," as they refer to it, than any of my troopers, who, to be honest, were only trying to keep up with my kill-rate. Hardly their fault, I suppose, if I'd trained'em to be super-competitive. And that was after I'd gained four In-Action promotions in three years. Was it three years? It all merges. I should have been upped to Battalion Chief, not dropped into "Pre-loved Independent Space Ships is Us", or PISS-U as the neon glare declares.

Run out of enemies, has it? The United Fed? They take me out my fighting role and get me fixing whichever ship comes in bent, buckled, burned-out, leaking and/or locking – when I should be fixing and firing V9 launchers, and 28-X systems loaded with Wipe-out Missiles. I ought to be leading troops in. Fed made an enemy outa me, alright.

***

Great! I'm conned and double-dumped. Must be four or five days since Smiler UV'd my face, judging by the stiff bits, dehydration and maggots. If I ever catch up with him, he's gonna get an image of me burned right through his cymbo-sucking face. I'm not one for forgetting.

An absolute age, and I'm coming round, start seeing again, stop retching and begin wondering how come my clothes are disarrayed, and where the shigh this turdrag dumped me. Stole my beautiful little Red Spirit ship – top of the range. If only she *were* mine, I'd have been long gone past Lumen, not puking up in some scrud and rock area outside the perimeter of some spaceport. Distant trees in a line… a rivercourse.

Two days wandering along the watercourse. The water was mostly in dry-bed pools, not running; and it was sour – some mineral in it. Just the minimum to drink. So I was getting in a bit of a state – wobble-legs and emaciation-wise. The settlement I came to was just a refuel, check-in and spares depot for small trader craft, mostly local. More of a beacon than a community.

Three guys and a woman ran the place. They all took a fancy to me. Bastards. Thirty-some days there. Around five or six craft calling in every day. They kept me locked up, though. So I didn't see much of the passing craft. It was every scrugging night with them – one or another – or all of'em at once. Turding pervs. I was on a chain and not much else. Till I got Emill with a throat chain – he might have been big and strong, but he was addicted to cymbo seeds, and crap at looking behind him. Good at dying, though. Didn't take him as long as he'd been fucking me up. But I got him on a permanent fuckup after about a half-hour's sheer choking agony round his throat.

Snidey Seeid was next. High-Ock fuel nozzle between his teeth and trigger on Full HP. He never said another foul-minded word, even when I tossed a flare into the spillage and he lit up like an 8D rocket. 'There, Snides, that's all *your* problems solved.'

Tragi and Yenni weren't silent with their bellies asunder, but there wasn't anyone else around to listen to'em, so their shrieking was like discola music to my ears. Sure, they suffered. They were supposed to suffer, after what they did to me, and saying I was a hard bitch inside and deliberately gloating over me, like Snides taught'em to. Three shighs and Yenni – remind me never to become a lesbian – it doesn't appeal, especially not the way Yenni believed in it. Huge turding mess they made all over the backroom floor.

The stench of spilled guts was almost enough to bury the aroma of cymbo mint that the place always whiffed of.

I suppose the good thing was any hoh-hah for me and the Red Racer was faded by then, and I took over the station for a time, seeing as there was nowhere to go. Perhaps three more deccas on my own, till this courier guy called Gurriah – Yeah, Gurriah the Worrier, he was called, so he said. He comes in with mail, essentials, pickups and two drop-off passengers. Assured that Emill and Scum were fixing something outback, he agreed to take me aboard and we lifted within the hour.

He was a randy shigher as well – but it was partly my instigation and we got on well enough in the hold, the engine room, control room and strap-down bed. Funny how his voice changed sometimes when we were in the bed. Like not him. He was another one where I picked up that slight acid-whiff of cymbo now and again. I'm going off it – makes me a touch nauseous.

Heffle! The time with Gurry went quick. I learned the stellography of half the cluster; and got memos of every language extant as far as Fringe West. Memos to understand them and speak them, with some read and write sections, too. Plus, that sweet little engine could be toyed with, tinkered, smoothed-up and speeded to shigh and back. 'Twenty-eight percent efficiency boost,' he said. 'Is what I've got out of it.' And he showed me how to do it.

Then one time, we were approaching Colva. 'It's my home planet,' he said. 'You really can't get to meet my wife.' And the control room went red, then black.

***

Shigh-alone knows how long later, I came round on some freighter where Captain Sylla and his three crew were apologetic, but they owed Gurry a favour – promising to drop me off three or four stops away from Colva. So in the meantime, how can you earn your keep, little lady? Hmm?

Shighing insatiable, they were, and one of'em sucked cymbo seeds. I was getting sick of them – bad feelings every time I smelled them but I got to know everything worth knowing about ally-life management. They were dealers in rarities in the living world, collecting, buying, transporting and selling everything from worm-sized seelo-caths to a pair of walwals that were the meat supply for a whole community on somewhere called Hrippsuth. They bred and grew at phenomenal rates. We only had the pair at the start – eighteen by the time I was sold off as their keeper.

That was an interesting time, life-managing on Hrippsuth. I ended up running the breeding research place. Funny, there, they were disappointed one time, hearing they wouldn't be getting any more supplies from Capn Sylla and his mini-dick trio. Seems the seelo-caths somehow escaped not long after I was dropped on Hrippsuth. I knew that tank seal wasn't reliable, especially with a liberal dose of arecetic acid poured down the back, where it couldn't be seen. Vicious little shighers, they are, burrow into anybody – much like *they* did with me.

I kept a little box of seelos in my pack, in case I needed them on Hrippsuth. Or anywhere else these days. It's like having your own little fun-pack.

‘Has she concluded the whole training cycle now?’ HighDoc Roeth checked the cubicle and its contents of one young woman on a strap-down bed. She wore a light indoor jacket now. *I preferred her naked*, he smiled. *So smartly-built, that little body. So satisfyingly so. But... all good things terminate eventually. There’ll be others.*

‘Indeed, she’s completed all fifteen full-immersion episodes.’ Sub Zackry waved the pad with all the checked-off details and conclusions. ‘Space mechanics… animal husbandry… military enforcement… navigation… Languages… the whole gamut.’

‘Hmm, she’s finished the whole programme in eighteen days – record for a woman.’

‘Not just for a woman: she’s equal with Gord Rook, and he’s still the best on active service.’ Zackry looked at the unconscious girl on the bed, pleased that his protégé had come through the training so well. *Not my place to skag on anyone, but Roeth’s been in there with her a few times – unofficially. And she’d been particularly irate, up-for-it and focused afterwards. Shigh – you shouldn’t have, Roeth, not with her aptitude and appetite for revenge.*

May the Gods help him if she realises what Roeth’s been doing to her while she’s been in her comatic state...

He stepped back, warmed to think of her – she was so good. An absolute triumph for the programme and for her as a person. *Her overall training score’s a record for anyone – huge top-mark score – full qualiffs in weaponry, construction, land craft, mining, agriculture, life management, personnel management...*

He sighed, *If I had a daughter, I'd be so proud if she was like you. You fully understand the cluster stellar layout, the various species-peoples from the cluster, their languages; every type of ship that ever sailed the vacuum. Shoiks, I admire you so much, to have come through it all so sparklingly.*

And so high on motivation. They don't come any higher on revenge quotient, either. Lorra! That was nasty, what you did with the mining duo. So richly deserved, though; beautifully designed, that episode, he congratulated himself. *And the crew at Emill's place got their just deserts.*

HighDoc Roeth was turning back to him, popping a cymbo mint in his mouth. 'What? *Sub*, are you saying I should watch myself? Eh? You think she might recall any of what might or might not have happened for real? She can't differentiate Real from Requence.'

'Exactly, Boss, she can't differentiate. You'd do well to remember that when she comes round for good.'

'Mind how you speak to me, *Sub* Zackry. She'll recall zilch. It means nothing to her. She gained vast experience – ten years of it, in two deccas.'

'She still holds vengeance close for groups of'em on Hrippsuth and Gallo. Good job the places don't exist. They'd be in deep if they did. Maybe you're in the same sub-folder as they are.'

HighDoc Roeth laughed. 'Open or shut, her eyes didn't see anything real – not the cubicle, the wiring, the staff. Or me. So worry for yourself, not me.' His cold stare was plenty enough to chill his subordinate.

'And never let her near anything that resembles Army Group Eight. Flag Sergeant or not, she'd wreak vengeance on every high officer in existence.'

They both smiled wryly at the thought. 'She only needs to go through the final aptitude and orientation programme—'

'We already know what her propensity is for—'

'She didn't have any choice in those situations, HighDoc. But in the reality periods, you really shouldn't have—

'Hush! I told you. And we have a fair idea of her strengths. I'm thinking in terms of her becoming the best Lead Colonist we ever graduated.'

'At least we're agreed on that.'

***

The world's blurred again – that pack of shighers did for me. I thought they were going to toss me off the top of that conrex tower we just finished building – merely because my bonus was double theirs. Must have been something in the drinks at the celebration top-out do. This is Recovery at the local Med Centre, is it? Am I back on that low-rise contract today? Tomorrow? I should be, but the way they went weird at the top-out hoosh-up...

No. No. I'm waking again. Lorra! that light hurts my eyes, piercing my brain.

I'm paralysed… fixed here, flat on my back – that's a ceiling… a different one. In a cubicle.

Ahh… my hands will move; I can flex my fingers. I feel down myself. I'm wearing a light jacket, cotone bottoms. I shivered... I'm sensing shadowy memories of times in this cubicle; a familiar voice wraithing around me… an aroma of cymbo mint…

I could do with some of the painex pills we developed with MedEx Inc. That was some time back – yonks ago. Good memories there. Lords! did we learn about medics, chemix. Huh – poisons and potions in equal measure. Right devious, pervy lot, they were, at MedEx. This place is so reminiscent of... something. I'm getting a whiff of cymbo, perhaps. Plain white room – loads of wiring and screens and no clothes in view... and wearing none until now...

Is this recovery? Or am I dumped in some medic-oriented situation again?

No. No, it's not a new situation. There's a voice. I know that voice. Telling me about the training. Training? '…the years around the planets have been modules to up-skill you…'

It means me. The voice is speaking to me. Saying it's not real? It shighing-well was real – ten years' worth of reality, whatever this eerie, dreary voice tells me.

They have another assignment for me?

'Your training is ended.'

They're pretending it's not real? That voice is lying to me. I know that voice. I recognise it. The times it murmured to me... the things it said. On the strap-down bed with Gurry... Things were happening to me. A person; a man – that cymbo aroma. It's him. Nothing I could do then.

But if now is a new reality...

Looking up and around with newly-opening eyes and mind…

Ah. Yes... That voice. That cymbo aroma.

You... I remember you.

What you did to me.

***

THERE'LL ALWAYS BE AN ENGLAND

Jaerd Williams, he was called by his mother, who thought Jaerd sounded Viking. Hard Jaerd, he was known as at St James' Park, and in the Wreckers' Arms, and in Millwall's Cold Blow Stand after the time he revealed his Newcastle colours at kick-off and sang and yelled abuse for fully two minutes before going down under four dozen home supporters.

He maintained his ferocious, unbowing attitude in whatever he did, so when he paused to rest part-way up the granite cliff-face, he automatically cursed, spat at a screeching seagull and looked at his already bleeding fingerends. 'Huh,' he grunted, not really caring. Sharp crystals filled some of the crevices and needed to be brushed away to get a good grip on the rock. Not accustomed to rock climbing, he wasn't well prepared to ascend from sea level to the top of the Land's End South Cliff. 'If it's not hard, it's not worth doing,' he told the unfazed seagull. 'So it'll take a bit longer than I thought.'

Steadying himself with a quick grab at the cliff-face, he shrugged, and watched the Atlantic waves crash against the sheer face below. With a sneer of disdain for the section he'd already conquered, he looked up at the next two hundred feet of looming walls of almost-bare weathered granite – a few sea thrifts lashed themselves in the wind. *So I might have a night out here. Hardly a problem.*

Beyond the towering face, a grey sullen sky threatened to drown the whole peninsula in torrential rain. A dismissive sneer consigned the threat to Jaerd's mental bin: *Nothing beats me*, he affirmed, *especially not a few drops of rain in some southern softie county.*

He was never sure why he did such things – cliff-climbing alone; first-ever bungee-jumper from half-a-dozen unlikely and dangerous bases; outscaring the other guy in a head-to-head on their Yamaha 850s. All part of the game. 'Game? It's life, man' he'd say. 'Got to do it, an't y'?'

'No,' said everyone else, and stood aside to watch Jaerd risk certain pain and likely death for some unknown reason.

'You got to, an't y'?'

His mother put it down to deliberately riding his bike into a brick wall when he was eight. 'No,' said his brothers, 'he was batchy long before that. Or he wouldn'a done it, would he?'

The five-minute break over, Jaerd began to move upwards again, collecting deep grazes on his knees and shins when he slipped, and slid back to the ledge he'd left ten minutes earlier. Badges of Pride, he thought for a moment, before turning back to the climb, and noticing the sky was darkening. *Too early for sundown; howay we go,* and he kept an eye on the gathering storm as he slowly recommenced the ascent.

And gather it did. Darker and more roiling as the minutes passed. *Might make a decent northern downpour*, he appraised, watching the inner churning of the dense clouds above. *They're getting bloody lower,* he told his latest feathered companion, with a tone of defiance that clouds would dare to do such a thing. *It's in a bit of a fettle up there, best get mi sen on the next ledge, and wait it out.*

Ten feet above, he wedged himself into a fissure that offered some protection from the direct wind and rain. *Way man! What's going on?* He watched the clouds, even lower, swirling angrily around the top of the cliff. In seconds, he was staring at violent, thickly-black billows that buffeted all around, him, reeking of dust and burning. Chokingly thick, swiftly covering him in a layer of filthy brown-black coarse dust.

'Y' don't drop no nukiller bombs on me and get away with it,' he swore at the sky, and the Russians and the Chinese… and Arsenal and Forest – whichever pack of much-hated underlife sub-humans had declared war on England.

'Y' don't fackin do that,' he cursed the unknown nuclear enemy under his breath, wondering if he was sucking in a mass of radiation with every intake of the foul air. 'Not to me, or Newcastle, or England, y' don't.' He paused, and re-arranged his mental list in reverse order, conceding that, above all, he was a rabid patriot for both places, and would defend both to the end, whatever anyone called him. The worse, the better. 'Fackin Chinks… fackin Ruskies… fackin Man United.'

Tucked in a narrow cleft, wedged between two columns of rock, salt-crusted, and now black dust-shrouded, he endured the night.

Come the slight lightening of morning, he flexed every muscle, and acknowledged that a) I'm real stiff, man, and b) yes, something really did happen up there yesterday. Rawking and coughing, he fetched a gubbin of black phlegm up and gobbed it towards a sorry-looking seagull.

'Wah man, wassis?'

A small line-fisher was chugging along, heading eastwards, sliding down the wave crests. Fifty metres out, pale blue, with tired timber and a white cabin surrounded by masts and antennae, it was making easy going with a following wind.

Behind it, a vast oval shape was gliding silently over the waves. Reaching from crest height to half-way up the cliff, the black-sheened mass hadn't been seen by the three crewmen on the Newlyn Sprite.

'It's a fackin UFO,' Jaerd instantly muttered. 'Bloody aliens done something up the top. Never did like that little ET shit.'

Keeping well back in his cranny, he watched, saw a point on the huge black shape glitter for a second, and the boat was gone in a whuff of light and an acrid wisp of smoke. The disturbed patch of water was lost in the wind in seconds.

Jaerd shrank back in wariness, feeling the blast of searing air reflected from the surface, bathing him in skin-scorching heat for a few cowering seconds. 'They're cauterising the coast,' he said. 'They better not have done Newcastle like this. Ma'll not be happy.'

Settling against the black-dusted rock, watching the enormous sateen oval continue its searing patrol along the cliffs, Jaerd began to plot his resistance strategy.

***

'The whole countryside has been levelled,' reported the pilot of a 737 who thought he was coming in to land at Heathrow, but barely made Amsterdam intact after a side-waft of scorching heat caught the plane in a violent updraught.

Recovering from his state of gibbering and the meltdown of half his plane, he expanded: 'London's gone… just flat and grey. Dust swirls… All the rest of the landscape, too. England's gone.'

***

The hastily-convened Euro-US Zoom conference brought a few facts and opinions together. 'Satellites confirm the overall picture: the whole British Isles archipelago has become one average, smooth, grey, dusty plain with frilly edges. It seems to be smoothed off to around a hundred metres above sea level. The

Irish Sea is being filled in, mostly with the Scottish and Welsh hills.'

'Vast machines roam back and forth across the land, shifting material in million-ton buckets, levelling it in swathes a mile across.'

'It's been a week, and the process seems to be virtually complete.'

'With no warning, the invasion and destruction of England has been total and absolute. The ruin extends across the whole of the United Kingdom and Ireland. It appears to be a force of vast alien creatures, each one being the length of a ship, with an array of appendages, arms, legs, breathing tubes, eye stalks, feeding orifices and anuses. Drones have sent back images, and so have satellites, although none remain active now.'

'We will call these beings the Groff, which is an approximation of the symbols on the side of a four-mile-long spaceship that landed three days ago. England and Scotland appear to be a mere landing area for the aliens. What was Wales is now the site of several dozen enormous buildings, perhaps for stores or accommodation.'

'And Oirland?' asked Dermot O'Guckin.

'Joined to Wales, and equally as flat as everywhere else. The same hundred metres above sea level, except for a few black and charred areas around the edges.'

'Oh,' he said.

'Mmm,' said someone called Douchêt, from Paris. 'I feel that our unified action must be inaction while we find out more information. We do not, ow you say, want them to look in zees direction.'

'The Russians sent several jets and a submarine to observe. They have disappeared. What we know now is that at least a dozen massive hovering craft are still patrolling the coast, and ravaging the cliffs and coastal villages with intense firestorms. The White Cliffs of Dover, for instance, are now glowing like a coke fire. We are confident that not a single person remains alive in England, or any of the other British nations.'

Other responses around the conference cameras varied, 'Ze UK? So vot?'

'Lil ole England, huh? Gee, that's a shame. That's in Lon-don is it? *Was...'*

'Gut. It save us a lot trouble.'

'So. We can fish where we want now, eh, Pablo?'

'Gee, that's a damn shame, we were taking a vacation there next year. It'll have to be New Zealand instead. Not a lot of difference, I gather.'

'Maybe we'a try to make rappresentazioni, molto circospettatamente. Very slowly – we don'a want it happening here, do we, eh?'

'кого черт возьми заботит,' the Russian delegate dismissed all concern on the matter, and mumbled to a colleague who was out of camera shot.

'Ça ne fait rien,' Douchêt le Douche muttered to his Belgian counterpart. They permitted themselves a brief snigger before re-assuming their pretence of sympathy.

'Busy bizz; busy bizz,' Project Manager Hluck cast a few dozen eyes over the screens. 'This new Way Point and Refuel Centre is coming along nicely,' he reported back to his company on Klagh Four. 'This planet has enough pre-salted water to last us several hundred years. The pumping stations on the western fringes of our base can extract plenty enough for our needs – up to twenty ships per day. And we have the central storage facilities alongside the ingress/egress strips. All are fully in place. No hitches. We can look forward with confidence.'

He relaxed – that was his twenty-eight-day set-up plan completed only one day beyond the scheduled time. 'Soon, every ship that refuels here will be sucking in millions of keelers of high quality ready-salted water every day.'

He was content; pleased, in fact. *Yes, most satisfactorily done; just a few details of tidying up and smoothing off to complete the whole operation. The InterStellar Inspection Team will arrive eventually, and issue their Certificate of Landing Worthiness, and permission to continue indefinitely. Wonderful.*

Yes... Soon as the Finishers arrive, the whole insignificant little corner'll be smoothed off to perfection. No matter, Inspector Bozuk's tame, and easily bribable, should there be any minor infringement that needs to be polished up later.

'Ahh. Bozuk's here early. Hardly had time to finish the tidying-up.' Project Manager Hluck bristled at the sight of the red striped InterStellar Inspection Ship, but remained confident that all was well – just another routine expansion development.

'Be fine, Boss,' Assistant One assured him.

‘Ahh.’ His bristles stood on end at the sight of the uniform heading in his direction. The inspector, yes. But a new uniform. ‘That’s not Bozuk.’ His wariness level rose, ‘We’ll need to watch this one, A1. He’ll be a stickler for something.’

The figure approached, ‘Ahh, a female inspector. Good. She’ll be no problem to break in to my way of seeing things… doing things. Pity, though, just when I’d got Bozuk eating out my pouch – a nod and a chink and he’d pass anything. Ahh, well… She looks very new; no experience. Soon put her right, eh, A1? How to do the job my way.’

The introductions were swiftly over. ‘Project Manager Hluck? I’m InterStellar Inspector Parlak. Shall we get down to business?

‘Now then, total area sequandered? Yes – checked off. Provisional permits for landing… yes. Initial permissions for constructions… Regulation distance between landing strips? Fine. Length of each? Well within rules. Starting times and dates? Hmmm… A little irregular there, hmm, PM Hluck? Native population displacement or removal – Total, right? Every single individual? Yes? Okay, that’s it, then, is it, Project Manager? You’re completed?’

‘Yes. That’s it.’ Hluck smacked his palps together in finalised pleasure. ‘There, then, I’ll be tidying up and preparing for my next Station Development – should be a big contract – with this one completed so neatly. Thank you, Inspector. You’ll be leaving before the darkness comes upon us, I expect?’

‘Oh no, Project Manager.’ ISI Parlak raised herself to her full elegant height, on all thirty-eight tarsi. ‘Just beginning, PM Hluck; just beginning. This has merely been your presentation. I have registered it, and will analyse everything, interpret all your evidence, and carry out my own inspection and investigation. Must do it all by the rules, you know. All by the rules. It's my report that carries the weight, not your submission.'

'But our usual inspector, Inspector Bozuk, always takes my word and evidence. He's perfectly happy to accept it as complete and correct, and to seal it with his approval. Then I tidy up any loose ends he's noted. It works very nicely.

'Hmm, I expect that's why he was un-integrated not long ago, hmm?' Inspector Parlak gazed into Hluck's eyes steadily, managing to back him down on all eighteen pairs.

'Un-integrated? Bozuk?' *My tame inspector, gone?*

'Indeed, probably fertilising a field on Far Fallins by now.'

'Er. Yesss… but…' He tailed off. In truth, he several-tailed off.

'Thank you. Your input is complete, PM. You told me that was it. Total. Completed. Thank you. I'll be in touch with any questions that arise in my queries, verifications and clarifications. I may need to be here some time.'

'Of course.' Hluck detected a puddle of perspiration forming under his top carapace.

'Ahh. Project Manager – so pleased to have found you. Continuing my enquiries, I'm afraid I do have one or two questions.' Inspector Parlak deliberately adopted her ominous tone; she hoped it would intimidate the confident Project Manager a little. 'Indeed, questions about possible discrepancies in the process you undertook.'

Undeterred by her tone, or whatever she thought she may have discovered, PM Hluck was confident he could explain anything or bluff anyone. Especially a new inspector, and a female one at that, unwashed behind the antennae. *Shame about Bozuk, though; he always saw things my way, especially down the barrel of a credit handover.*

'Original permissions and/or notifications?' she began. 'The indigene population? I see no evidence that they were given the obligatory notice of impending clearance.'

'The NIC? Well… I, er…' He made a show of sorting through documents, wallets, screens and pads… 'Must have mislaid them.'

'In which case,' Inspector Parlak ostentatiously made a few notes on her Phi-pad… 'Failure to…' she murmured loudly as she wrote. 'In which case we must resort to the alternative permissions – the final declaration by the last remaining indigene, hmm? The ultimate permission must be a declaration by the last native who lived here uninterruptedly between the initial arrival, and the validation of the permission. You do have such a document, I presume?'

'Of course. Everything is in order. I'll tidy them up. I didn't think you'd want to see the details.' Hluck breathed easier. *This won't be too difficult. You think I'm a fool? We spent the last few days creating exactly what you want. An easy matter of rewording the last survivor's shrieks and declarations. All that screaming and chanting had been its ultimate surrender to our promptings. Merely been a matter of uprooting the most relevant sections, and creating a few extras. Simply a case of assembling them into a cogent message of handover. All completed a day ago. It always worked, and slotted so neatly into Inspector Bozuk's records.*

'You have the audios? the visuals? In-depth Ongoing Scans? No need to tidy it all up. If it's in there, I'll find it. I'll take everything. *Now.*'

Hluck didn't move. 'Inspector Bozuk never—'

'*Now*, Project Manager,' She repeated.

Hluck capitulated, smirking internally. 'It's er, yes… a single individual we knew was still on the project site—'

'What? You had not actually completely cleared the site of all indigenous sentient life when you began the project? One of them remained on site throughout the entire period of the development work? And nor had you gained pre-permission? This could be serious, PM Hluck, hmm?'

'Er, actually…' Hluck was thinking furiously, *damn inspector twisting everything. Let her have it all. It's all there.* 'Yes, we have all the records for you, haven't we, A1? Can you bring them for the inspector? Rather unsorted as yet… but the survivor could—'

'What! It still lives?'

'No. Unfortunately, it – a male – died yesterday, despite our best efforts. The carcass? No – incinerated with the regular rubbish.'

'And it was present throughout the development?' Parlak checked.

'Yes. We had sporadic sightings of evidence – items moved, taken… It seems he was surviving very tenaciously on ocean fish and vegetation. He had been climbing on a vertical edge of the project site, at an extreme fringe location. He was missed in the original wipe-away and subsequent cauterisations—'

'Rather careless of you, hmm? It sounds to have been tenacious, indeed.'

'He was eventually captured, much below what we understand to be the normal dimensions of size and weight… er, he was eating berries… grain, found water. We retained him for just such a purpose. And yes, of course, he willingly agreed to cede his former land area to we Foy'ghats. It's all in the scans and ultrecords. A1 has it all.'

'Including his LT brain scan at the time of his agreement to it? It must be shown to be voluntary.'

'Naturally. It's all there.' Hluck sighed his relief. *All neatly fashioned since the creature was taken. Of course, we knew what the inspector might demand. So it's ready.*

'Bring it to me in its entirety,' Parlak ordered. 'With all the recorded evidence of its agreements, and proof of continuous residence.'

'Of course, Inspector.' Hluck underwent a moment of triumph, *The creature did as it was forced to do, under the drugs and pain obligators.*

'So, creature. You're the centre of this matter, are you?' ISI Parlak studied the amalgamated re-living of the final surviving human land-occupier. The hologram lay there. Unclothed. Strapped to an elevated surface. ‘You’re so tiny. Insignificant, almost. And yet sentient. And intelligent, judging from other similar beings I observe on this planet?

‘Leave me with all this, Assistant One. No, I don’t need help with interpreting or analysing. Thank you, A1. And goodbye.’

So she settled comfortably, and set about obtaining and analysing the creature’s declaration that, as the sole native of the lands that had been sequandered, he had willingly ceded the area to the Foy. As the last survivor, who had been there in continuous residence since…

Yes… yes… it’s all there. But, delving deeper… *Hluck had erected barriers within; curtains that hid screaming agonies and confusion. So much tangled and shrieking agony… the need for peace within. For an end to it all.* Despite all this, Inspector Parlak checked that the being knew what he was doing, that he accepted the newcomers’ right…

Yes, yes. It’s all there. Hluck has it all correct. She sighed through every spiracular orifice. *But it doesn’t feel entirely true. This determined creature gave it all up willingly?*

Pincering a few drinks open, she ruminated on the matter. *Hluck just has that attitude. He’s not following the rules: he’s created this to persuade me. Does this chime true? Is it a little too organised? In too much the correct format, considering the post-event nature of the whole concession. How much of this was willing? How coerced was it? How much had been manufactured by Hluck's team? Reassembled from a mass of non-compliant communication from the thing?*

Directly, with her own vast mind, Inspector Parlak probed into the tiny recesses of the ultrecords and living scans of the last survivor of these lands – of TM Hluck's Landing and Refuelling Base – the Way Station.

'I hear you, little creature. What are you saying in there? You locked yourself away, did you? Imprisoned yourself in your own mind? For safety? For escape from pain and death?

'Let me listen to you, creature. Let me ease in. Yes… I have more skill at this than an untrained project manager.' Gradually, Parlak teased aside the curtains inside the dead human's mind, within the recreated ultrecords. It's there, isn't it, Little One? Yes… yes. I hear your voice within… Let me in.' *Some kind of regular, melodic pattern to the internal speech? An imperative within. Your core belief endlessly repeated. As though by recitation. What are you saying in there? Come on… come on… let me hear.* "There'll always be an England while there's a country lane…" So strong within. Strident defiance. An agony of willpower. "There'll always be an England…"

This is not compliance; it's by excess force and reconstitution of meanings. Not by agreement. I need to speak with Hluck about this matter. 'A1! Come here at once.'

***

‘You fool,’ Hluck towered high over the still-recumbent ISI Parlak, ‘You millocular imbecile; coming here, all nodules and notepads; flashing your nemi szervek everywhere.’

Looking to Assistant One for support, he pursued his attempt to intimidate the new inspector. ‘It is all there. And correct. The things it had previously cherished and clung to in its final darkness. Those things it chanted? Mere inbred, embedded compulsions. Automatic utterances.’

Completely unphased by Hluck’s ranting, Inspector Parlak smilated to A1 for having to put up with his bullying project manager. She clearly recalled what she had seen and experienced in trawling through the mind and memories of the now-dead denizen of these lands. Through pain-slitted eyes, the ravaged face had seen the vast bulk of Hluck and his team, hovering and crowding over him as they tortured and shrieked into his mind, demanding and twisting, forcing.

Dozens of stalks of eyes… writhing things that came and probed and flickered and glowed.

“You’re just mile-long millipedes. Fackin aliens. Y’ can bugger of – I’m English.” And the tiny creature had retreated into its own core being, seeking and finding refuge, reinforcing its own Land Oath with its chanted song, “There’ll always be an England.”

‘Inspector Bozuk would never have—' Hluck changed tack, ‘Yes, all those things. There was no country lane any longer… no cottage, no fields of grain. All is gone. The whole of its land was long-since flattened; it was all resonated to uniformity; dusted for a thousand kreet in all directions. That creature’s *England* is no more.’

Parlak recalled delving inside the mind of the little being, so carefully, reading, seeing, sensing… "While ever there's anyone proud enough to call himself English… You've no idea what it means, y' fackin alien shits. To feel the chains of real loyalty of mind and soul. You got no soul, you insectoid monsters… Y' not English. So piss off, y' shouldn't be here.

"I shouldn't be here – I ought to be smashing up the terraces at Elland Road or City Ground. I want my England back."

'Ever and again, Project Manager Hluck, that last surviving resident of these lands returned to its core belief and message. This is what it really believed and wanted. Nothing else. "There'll always be an England, while there's a country lane. Wherever there's a cottage small, beside a field of grain."

'And these things it named, I've carried out research among the minds of other denizens of this planet. I understand what is meant. Do they exist any longer?'

'No. Certainly not,' Hluck was slipping into pre-panic mode. 'We're finalising the last remnants of the original surface—'

'So! The last remnants? How long after you assured me that all was finished and smoothed? But, you say, there might be something remaining, then?

'Cease all operations! Bring me recorded evidence of all clearancing since my arrival. Stop *everything* while I check this whole project site. *Now!'* She pressed the Priority Notification button, *'All activity to cease as from Now.*

'I have discovered a small area, PM Hluck, which happens to be at exactly the mean level of the newly-levelled plane, and which has not been affected; it is *still* the original surface. Some original features remain there, including what we believe was spoken of – chanted compulsively by your last sole survivor.

'There is a narrow thoroughfare… a small dwelling… and a patch of a crop know as barley. These constitute the essential features of your contract with the creature – that this land would remain his, known as England, while there is a country lane, a small cottage, alongside a field of grain – which barley is.

'Therefore,' she concluded, 'the erstwhile England does still exist. Thus, this development is illegal.'

'But, but… The area you point to is smaller than a single ship. It would have been eradicated by now, had you not—'

'But there are other areas of original surface, PM Hluck, scattered fragments of items from the original surface – very much destroyed, smithereened and levelled. Kreet after kreet of it, levelled.

The creature's consent should have been obtained before the project commenced—'

'But, we would have no way of knowing which would be the last.'

'Irrelevant. In advance, any inhabitant would have sufficed. At a pinch and a twist, you could have made very sure that all was totally finished, and then extracted consent immediately afterwards, as a Fate Agreed, from the sole remaining native. But definitely not during the clearancing, and this project was clearly not actually completed, was it? As you assured me it was. And at that stage he clearly did not agree – not deep down, regardless of what assemblages of words you concocted for him to have supposedly spoken.

‘Where is your team of Finishers – double-booked them somewhere else, did you?’

‘But Inspector Bozuk—’

‘Was un-integrated, remember? For collusion in just such matters. Hmm?’ She stared up at the slightly sagging Hluck, focusing every eye-stalk and audi-node on him. ‘I have researched these matters – and have concluded that these are the archetypal images of this island. They epitomise what this land once was.

‘At the risk of repeating myself – but you do not seem to be grasping this – You have not eradicated all trace – every person, every vestige of surface.’

‘Mere chance, Inspector; the survivor was located within a peripheral fringe of the region. It avoided all efforts to kill it, remove it—'

‘And the areas of pre-existing landscape that are still there?’

‘Scarcely more than a single one; as you say – less than the size of a ship, Inspector Parlak. Sheer chance of being at the exact median level of the new surface. A mere oversight, a slight delay.’

‘On such things do empires hang, Project Manager… Assistant One.’ Inspector Parlak adopted the placid, philosophical point of view. Despite herself, she felt a tinge of pleasure at her competent handling of this case.

‘But it was simply overlooked in our pressing need to create the Way Station. So minor. Surely…?’

‘But it flouts InterStellar law – “If NO survivors…” and “NO trace of previous…” And there again, “Complete and unambiguous agreement.” Yet you have failed on all counts – a survivor, whom you killed illegally, as he had survived the killing time and was into the reconciliation time. A blatant attempt to force a concessionary gift of the land to you. His dying words, apart from the period of shrieking gurgling screams, of course, were, "There'll always be an England... while there's a country lane..."' she checked her notes... '"wherever there's a cottage small beside a field of grain."

'It's all perfectly clear enough. He was alive when the concessionary period began, and his view should have been the dominant one. Indeed, it should have been sought and agreed much earlier.'

'Yes, but, surely—'

'Yes, but nothing. You failed on several counts. You had no initial permission or invitation to commence the work here—'

'Inspector Bozuk always allowed me to file the permits later, as part of the handover package.'

'I'm not him; and you're only compounding your guilt by constantly referring to a dead criminal.'

Hluck eyed her up – three dozen eyes focusing hard down, trying to decide how to proceed. *Is she bribable? Would I get away with ripping her head off in an accident? Huh – it would probably regenerate. She's still going on* '...survivor entering the reconciliation period... torturing and executing him whilst attempting to extract dying concessions from him. You completely ignored, or chose to misinterpret, his sworn wishes. You even allowed the physical focus of his Land Oath to still exist in some part.'

She summed up, 'Because you recorded and submitted his dying words, they become the basis of future application of IS law in this specific case, and to me, they clearly indicate an utter refusal to concede this land to you, or anyone else. "There'll always be..."

'I shall be open to your proposals of how you will make restitution to this planet.'

Three separate minds pondered the difficulty. One patiently awaiting the answer that was needed. Another hoping his boss would be executed. And the third one twisting and wriggling for a cheap way out, if bribery and violence were definitely off the agenda.

'I understand,' Hluck began, 'that there were large numbers who were indigenous to this area, but not actually present at the time of our intervention. We could compensate them… rehome them somewhere—'

'Utterly insufficient.' Inspector Parlak broke in, *You arrogant smirker.* 'IS rulings and precedents indicate that Article 19; Para 9zero7 is invoked in such cases. The complete re-creation of the original landscape and peoples here.'

Hluck blanched.

'And the offending party would need to seek elsewhere for a different IS Way-point. Another planet. Hmm?'

'But… but… The entire project? Returned to…? You mean start again?'

'Mmm, yesss. Elsewhere, Project Manager. I see no future for your project here. This is a viable planet, not one to be recklessly drained of its most vital natural resource – the salt water. And the destruction of a particularly vibrant land area.'

'I… but…' His glittering eyes were fading in the doom-pit into which he was sinking.

'This planet has the potential to become a full Galactic Member—'

'Full? But they're tiny. So easily—'

'Thank you, Project Manager. There are choices to be made here – particularly if you expect a future? Or push up the Day-Zizz alongside Inspector Bozuk? As you choose. Hmm?'

Choices? A glimmer of hope? Hluck's antennae perked slightly.

'On the one claw, officially, the whole region of the project should be time-jumped back to immediately before your intervention, as though it had never happened.'

'But, all these lands that turned into runways and storage depots? The whole archipelago?'

'Yes. Think what the alternatives are. The whole planet?'

'But time-jumping the whole planet back forty days would put it out of synchrony with its solar system – disturb the whole balance of all the planets. Utter chaos.' Hluck's eye-stalks gyrated.

'Indeed, so…'

'What? You want me to time-jump the whole solar system? It would be virtually impossible… the repercussions would be…' He was backing into the pit of doom.

'Indeed so. Bearing that in mind, let's talk about what might be practical – the restoration of only the most directly affected land mass, then? This England? And the adjacent areas?'

Hluck managed to suck in a little air; the possibility of continuing life glimmered. *Dare I mention the expense? Perhaps not... considering...* 'And that would involve?' he tentatively enquired.

'I could agree to a simple time-jump back for only this area. Forty days. To immediately prior to your arrival.'

A hundredth the expense of the whole planet... a ten-millionth the cost of the whole solar system – the company would kill me if that happened. 'Yes, I could perhaps reset the time for these lands.'

'Oh, good,' Inspector Parlak murmured. 'And the one hundred and eighty cubic keelers of sea water must be restored, of course.'

'That really is impossible, Inspector… it's spread half-way round the galactic arm by now.'

'Hmm, indeed so. Perhaps purchase some from other sources?' She enjoyed the cross-antennaed look on his peri-calyx. But, a touch of almost sympathy, 'Or you might make some other direct recompense to this small area of land?'

'Like what?'

'Give them something of value? You must have a few orbital craft you could leave for them? Some communications equipment? A T&S re-timer? Starburst computer? One of your smaller IS craft, hmm? Just a little something to give them a boost, help them out into the rest of the galaxy, hmm? As recompense for the inconvenience, hmm?'

'But if I put them back pre Day 1, they'll have had no inconvenience.'

'Project Manager,' she readopted her excessively patient-but-very-ominous tone. 'They'll have missed out on forty days of their own world history. That may take some huge psychological toll on them – especially as the rest of the planet is aware that they were wiped out for forty days, and have suddenly reappeared. How would you feel if everyone thought you were dead, and you came back, totally unaware, baffled, and having no idea where you had been, or what's happened in your absence?

'Just a few little boosters to sweeten them, hmm? Some goodwill gifts, hmm? And we'll regard the matter as settled, hmm?'

Hluck sighed, cursed and sagged, imagining the vast amount of trouble and expense that loomed… the indignity… the shame. But, to survive, it would have to be done. He rustled his thoracic plates in fury and turned to get on with it – the sooner, the cheaper.

Inspector Parlak watched him depart, her palps almost glowing with satisfaction. There: one major infringement successfully dealt with on my first assignment. "The rules exist and must be followed," as my tutor always told me, 'but measure them with a glass of humility – there but for the grace of the Endless Manitau, remember, young Parlak.'

And, I think, these restored lands should prosper with Hluck's selection of gifts – such fierce pride deserves to succeed. Give them an edge among their own neighbours here. Huh, not so much as a whimper of support or protest from any of them. Yes, this England's leadership should earn this planet a place at the galactic assembly in due course.

Plus, I have a tame project manager who won't try to slash corners again, especially if I remain here a time, and keep an eye on the restitution.

Yes, a most satisfying first inspection.

***

Jaerd paused in his ascent, gazing down into the crashing Atlantic waves for a few moments. *Whoa –*

what was that? A touch of dizziness made him shake his head.

He blinked hard a few times, and waited. *Nothing.* And continued his determined way, unconcerned by anything other than the climb ahead.

THEY TOLD ME TO STAY

They're in the bubble with me! Mikita. Weapons flashing. From behind. *Where the Naid they come fro—?*

I'm down. Crashing all over me, yacking and rawking. Grabbing at me. I got no weapon – *I'm an observer for shikesake. So how'd I not see them?* I'm crushed down. Claws at my throat and eyes. Huge strength. Mouths and nostrils flaring. Whole faces snarling on me. I'm down and out flat. *How's this happened? What the shike's happened? How? Inside my own obs bubble! Must have de-coded the doors. And silenced them. Never heard a beep, much less the klaxonic clamour there should'a been.*

Fighting and struggling like shike but I'm down from the off, and barely even twitching under all of them. Shike I'm caught. I'm done.

Something techno over my face. I'm freezing up. Slowly. Paralysed. Screaming inside. I'm captured. *How the Hagra?* Can't believe it. Mind spinning, jabbing – *How did they get anywhere close? Base team's got my back. Must have us on cameras and sensors.* I'm fully protected. *Unless they been wiped out?* The shame of being subdued so quickly, so easily… *I'm fading off… Shi—*

***

Waking up. Pain everywhere. Eyes raging stinging. Somebody's here. *Wass appnin?* I'm trying to demand. *Baffled. Can't understand. My forward observation bubble was perfectly disguised. How the naid did you find me?* Bubble was completely hidden. Undetectable. I'm forward lookout on Calinkyor – one of a dozen moonlets orbiting Koti. Sure, we're taking a chance being there, but no real likelihood of being detected. And it provides twice-daily overlooks of their main base.

Species. Gender. Name. Rank. Number – is all I give… 'Human. Male. Alika Honi. Sergeant Guardian. 90876.' If I tell'em that, they have to tell me who they are. Where from.

Except they don't – just slickering jibbers and clacking at me and all round me. They must not mistreat me. Are obliged to feed me.

Sure they will.

I'm sort of coming round… see a bit. I'm in our own Back Base. A dozen Mikita I can see, yickering and squacking and jabbing at me. This's *our* control room. Should be four of our backup and coordination team guys in here every shift. *Shikerty – it's stripped bare. All sealed up. Official seals. It's been abandoned. Closed. By our lot. I been deserted – They told me to remain here. Then shiked-off and left me. The shikers, the team's left me!* Can't have been urgent – they would have blown it up, not stripped and sealed everywhere.

I'm staring round. They're yippering and demanding at me, smacking at my face – sharp claws they got. 'Piss off,' I tell'em. *So why'd they desert me?* Must have thought I'd been seen, and the Mikita were heading my way. 'Stay there,' my orders had been. *'Stay there.'* So they had to leave me there, or the Mikita would have been tipped off. It was weak, but the best I could think off without screaming and ranting and changing sides. It had come straight from Captain DA'vid himself, 'Stay there.'

Not that there's any real "sides" in all this… Koti's a border planet where Terra Federation's expansion meets Mikita Territory – their Empire, or Commonwealth or Realm – we hadn't had enough discussions with them to find out. Mostly, it was minor clashes, probably rooted in misunderstandings when we first encountered each other. Jealousies and prior claims led to bigger clashes. I expect some incidents were arranged by one side or the other. Or just natural, like this one, where we'd dared to land an observation team. Viz: me and the backup team in Base, all secure and safe, just watching their main colony and military base with a mass of sensors; monitoring all the data. I stream it all to Base, the other side of Calynkor. They blip it back to SHQ, and look out for me. Or not. *I'm a statistic – Presumed Dead. Ordered to remain. Overrun. KIA.*

They're looking and sounding shiked off with the empty Base and me. Clawed us both up a bit and I'm going in Trance Outta Here Mode and not letting'em get in my head…

Looks a fine planet down there: chlorophyll based, with oxygen, water, the lot. Abundant native life across varied topographies and ecosystems. Pity they'd found it first: it was a salient deep into our realms. Made it uncomfortable for us. Terra Federation probably couldn't allow it to continue. But that's hardly my decision to take. Merely an eye, that's me.

Used to spend my auto-rest time in the Bubble asleep or gazing at the holos of my wife and the baby on the inside of my bubble bunk – *Such blonde hair they have, blue eyes... the same smile.* We had pseudo conversations, but they were a bit restricted with three-unis-old JUddy; and MAzzy and I had said the same things a thousand times already. Real and pseudo.

Time had been stretching a bit, getting uncomfortable – my replacement should have returned seventeen shifts earlier with supplies. Instead, all I got was 'Remain there. Direct order from the captain – *Stay.*' Like you tell your pet koira. I remember seeing his face staring at me out the screen. I didn't like him at all – it was him who'd been joking about the holo of my MAzzy. Crude shiker – saying things like that about somebody's wife. But I've been getting too low on food; oxygen running out. My air was stale. Condit unit chugging ominously; power settings near zero.

Orders should be updated daily. *'Stay there,'* was the last order. Direct command – martial court for any disobedience, with the inevitable verdict that officers rely on to enforce their will. Then the sets went into Mute, and nothing I could do about it – strict ether silence, even on tight beams fully coded. Sure I could have left in the hoverbug – but they're detectable, and desertion's a mandatory, execution offence. They knew where I was. So I had to carry on with my duties and try to get some messages through as part of my routine blip-reports. It made sense now – They were busy dumping me.

***

The Mikita took me off Calinkyor eventually. Trussed up. Bagged. Zero-sound helmet clamped on. Spiral zip craft down to the surface of Koti by the feel of it. Made a note for future ref.

***

I was in confinement for… I dunno. Long time. Mostly on my own. They came in my cell – bare like a medic's sairaala room. They'd bring equipment in. Talk at me. Take blood and samples of whatever. It really yiking hurt sometimes, and if I resisted they strapped me down and did their sample-taking anyway – blood, skin, tissue, bone, whatever – and padded off. *Guess they don't believe in anaesthetic.*

Or they'd take me in other rooms and strap electro-masses all over me. I stopped struggling cos they dragged me if I fought. And my arm was broken doing that and they fixed it. Not gentle. But there was plenty of time for it to heal… ages. Really – *ages. They've deserted me, total.*

Mostly, it was one that called itself Van Kilan. Or *herself*, she told me, and blushed through the non-scaly skin patches on her face. Naid-alone knows why she'd blush – it's hardly embarrassing to state your gender. *Maybe it is for them.* I studied her. *Never been especially fond of lizardy things. Perhaps she's trying to be nice.* I dunno. *It's not working.* She was scary. Pointed teeth and a tail that whipped when I wasn't doing something how she wanted. Like a serrated top edge, her tail had. That was scarier than her teeth.

***

Didn't see any other people – not human-people, anyway, in all that time. Loads of Mikita in uniforms and formal attaché-style. Occasional visitors, bit jerkier than the Mikiti, more feathery than scaly, but similar. They all talked with me, at me. In Stang, sort of, though I learned quite a bit of Mikita. Gradually, we got by – pretty fluently, actually, me and them.

No torture, no overt brain-washing I was aware of – and I'm not stupid about such things. They did knock me out sometimes, though, and I'd come round thinking my head was bursting with pain. Must have been probing me, cos I was thinking about Terruusi, where I come from, and MAzzy and JUddy. Jeems, I longed to be back with them – *Naid! I need some warmth of humanity, and a change of conversation* – I used to get sick of talking vectors and sensors, whores and booze with the other troopers at Back Base. Now I'm liitu'd-off with avoiding talking about such things when the Miki prompt and probe me. *How big's JUddy now? How's the new spread coming along? MAzzy's brother, too: has he been drafted yet? Was MAzzy pregnant when I left? Wonder if I have another little girl, or a boy now?*

The other peoples – with fluffy feathery bits – I saw one naked once when they were taking me down a corridor – in a side room. Feathered pube! Jeem! Anyway – they're called Lintuja. And they're an ally or friends-with lot. Not sure if they're from different planets or the same ones. *Doesn't matter, I suppose. Not to me. Not for a long time now.*

They got slacker with me. Days doing nothing. Let me go in a lounge where there were other Miki. Singles or pairs. *Must be a library or games-rec room.* But I decided the other Miki in there were prisoners, too. Maybe crims or troopers on punishment confinement. Whatever, they didn't mix much, not with each other, and sure not with me. So I mooched and poked and tried the screens and managed to get into some viddy channels and info banks. The infos went off after a few deccs. *I suppose y' don't want me doing that, huh? Stop me learning too much?* Van Kilan was in there the first few times, but soon took to just pushing me in and leaving me to it. So I watched the other Miki and the vids and the live channels. And I memo-dropped loads of vids and catals, banks on all kinds of things. The memos pow-dropped and my brain sort-of played them slow afterwards, probably while I was asleep. *Know thine enemy*, was my total maxim.

It got so I could understand what they were saying nearly all the time – even the other Miki in there when they talked together. They were basic troopers on sick patrol. Been somewhere – they wouldn't talk about it – and were here for a few deccs L&R before doing whatever else they did. Funny lot, some of'em. Funny-narky with me, like something was my fault. But funny-jokey with anybody they knew well. Had to know'em well, though. Took'em time to speak with anybody they only met a decc or two back, much less do one of the vidi-games with someone new.

I scoured the channels for news – got some. No mention of conflict of any kind with TerraFed. So I was really getting it in my head that I was forgotten – Presumed Dead. *PD on the reports, that's me. Probably just one report – filed in the banks and forgotten. Fading even with MAzzy, I expect.*

Didn't do much for my morale. It was getting hard to keep focused. On my own like that. Had a time when I got really depressed and had a lot of fighting going on inside me. Funny – Kalin was sort of softer then – like not japping at me so much. And didn't drag me or zap me.

Dunno why – buck me up, or given up, I dunno – but I got some different time out, not in the lounge. This was in a place like a canteen, but without all the rowdy clatter and raucous conversations that humans do in canteens. It was like quiet murmuring and slickerty scratching in there. Still didn't see any other humans. All Mikita and a few Lintuja. Van Kilan led me to a screen and pad with a wall-board. 'What you want?'

I looked at the board. The menu. *'Lihapiirakka ja sipulit herneitätold,'* I told her, pointing, without much idea what it was, apart from meat and veg of some kind, and feeling over-rushed. She looked – I think – a bit surprised that I said it about right, and told me where to sit: at a table and she'd bring me the food.

Two mins and she joined me, and parked herself opposite Tried to smile, I think. She seemed nervous. But the place was quiet, a few others coming in. Lots of room. We went a few times, maybe a decc between one and the next. I sort of looked forward to them – made a change, watching someone new, even the Miki. Learned a lot.

Then this time, the place was getting filled-up and some Mikita came and parked themselves at our table – nodded at Kilan and hicked at me, and said something about the food. They looked familiar – *I can even tell one from another nowadays – you're in the games lounge sometimes,* I thought. The food they were saying about was kalaa and siruja – locally caught, according to the menu board – I entertain myself reading their stuff on walls and covers of document wallets – and screens, too. I splashed plenty of etikka on the kalaa, like some of them do. The kalaa was good, actually, like battered fish. Oh, and with a big glass of oranssa that Kilan always insists I drink. Must be something in it, I suppose, but they get brutal if I don't cooperate over that.

They – the other non-uniformed Miki – asked about me. Kilan said it was okay for them to speak to me. *This is very different; they're not military or formal – maybe public, or just general office workers or casuals. I'm almost mixing with non-official personnel.* I could talk with them okay – a few spoke Stang, but not Terruus. And my Mikita was better than passable, though a bit sing-song, I gathered. I have a quaint *maatila aksentti*, apparently – reminds them of the farmlands. They're amused by it. So I cultivate it – that's my joke – *cultivate* my yokel accent. I think they're entertained – it's not easy to tell through all the mandible bristles.

Van Kilan was nervy through all that meal, but she took me again a few days later. And it was the same – I could choose which foods I wanted. But not drinks. I had to have the oranssa. They had beer which smelled good.

Then one time when Kilan took to sitting at another table, somebody pushed his beer my way and shut one eye – He yiking winked at me! So I tried it. *Jeems, this is good stuff.* I could have slurped the lot, but I saw Kilan bristle. So I thanked my benefactor after another quick swallow. He's a guy with a sprinkle of blue scales on his neck, like a sage lizard's dewlap. But these were smooth and had a metallic sheen. Maybe it was the beer, but I thought he looked quite smart.

I was put into another cell that looked like an independent apartment away from the block where I'd been kept all that time. I could go out with Kilan at first, looking round, conditional on me peomising to drink the oranssa, 'It is necessary for your well-being,' she said. The area I was allowed to explore was the compound – like an army camp cum hospital.

Van Kilan was making sure I could find my way back to my apartment, I suppose. It was easy enough. I was familiar with the layout from my time in the Bubble. I'd seen this site from orbit so many times. Military camp with its own living, working and recreation facilities, a town surrounding it, and farming lands extending to the mountains one way and the coast the other. Plus spreading into grasslands in every other direction.

Simple, once you got the idea the complex was laid out in external tangential circles – kissing circles, we called'em back home. There were open gateways from one to the next, but they didn't have gates or guards. So it was problem-free to move around.

Is this why I was ordered to wait? 'Stay there', they'd said. No misinterpreting that. Direct must-obey order. Did they expect me to be taken, not killed? To find things out at closer quarters? Well, I'm following orders right enough. Just going on longer than they expected. Can't say I'm not loyal – still observing, remembering.

***

One night I wasn't locked in. I didn't hear the outside bolt thunk into place, and I realised. So I went out, to look round on my own, on foot, in the dark. I just wandered under dim orange lights. Took directions I hadn't been before. Couldn't remember details of what was what or where from when I'd been orbiting up there – but it had been so long ago. My head hurt if I went near some places, or maybe some people. But other places were open – like a bar, and a caff-diner like a Uniweb Communics place where some of them were hooked up. I talked a bit with other people. A kid who shouldn't have been out that time of night split his knee open and I pressed the skin back and held it in place and muttered at him, and got bluish blood all over my hands.

I even got a drink. Beer. Whole one to myself. No idea how – *baarimikko* just pushed one my way and waved my protest away when I asked about paying. He pointed to my wrist bangle with the timer and monitor – *I suspect it does all sorts.*

Several times after that, I wasn't locked in. Giving me more freedom, huh? Should do it in the day. I ain't nocturnal, y'know. *Maybe I'd see too much in daylight?* The hurting became less common, as well. Then, I dunno, I was going out, just sort of enjoying freedom and learning and relaxing like uncontrolled. Lasted a time – good few deccs. *They haven't said anything about it, but they must know and not mind. They let me get food and a drink in little bars in a couple of back-streets.* Quiet, murmuring places with low red lights and twinkly music. Warm and got plants potted all round and the viddy on. Locals sometimes talk with me – about some game on the viddy, or the beer, or some sexy creature… *Sexy? A lizzie?* But it's almost like okay – sitting in a bar with a dish of something wriggly-cooked, a game on, a beer. *My own beer!* – 'You have creds on your wrist bangle,' one *baarimikko* said.

***

Sitting there in the Plough and Howitzer one evening, same as a dozen previous occasions, and the doors crash in. Gang of'em in silver-black uniforms. Rampaging all over me like in the Bubble on Calinkyor, all jippering and ranting and head-smashing claws. Got me down on the yiking floor and battering at me and I didn't know what— *Maybe they only just found I keep going wandering, and drinking beer. And watching vidds of all kinds… and the kynsi pallo games… uncontrolled chattering with locals. Demonic stuff, huh? But I been drinking the oranssa, like they really insist. Didn't try to cross them up.*

Woke up sometime later. Much later, by the crusty state of the mess I was in – plastered in shit, rips and bruises, back in my little cell dump again. Back in the block house. *Square One,* I call it – *twelve by twelve.* Lights on. Alone. For an age. Days, it must have been.

Two came in, wanting something. Demanding. I wanted to clean up. No chance. So it was no cooperation from me. They didn't like that. Got a cuff in the face from a heavily irate Mikita. Still couldn't clean up. Deep in do-do's, mostly my own. *Exit freedom's first bloom,* I thought. *How yiking ignominious, lying here. Legs killing me… bruises everywhere. Stiff and bleeding.*

Nothing in the room to clean myself with. Bed too clean to lie on. What the shit? I don't do the cleaning, so I crawled onto the white sheet and powed out, feeling really chissed off with TerraFed. 'Stay there,' they'd told me. And with the Mikita for locking me up… for… Naid-alone knows how many years now. And shiked off with hurting, being under everybody's unguis, being miserably alive… 'Naid'em,' I said. 'I'm out of here.'

It hurt, starving myself and not drinking. They brought some stuff for me. Including the oranssa. It went straight down the slop. Rubbed shit on the food. One lost his luonne and gave me a thorough pasting in the mess I'd made. Lost some teeth then, I think. Hardly mattered. 'Gonna die,' I told the next one who came strutting in. 'Sore losers, y'are…'

They didn't like being losers – bit sore about it. So they strapped me down and forced more oranssa down me, and hosed me down with the coldest water I've ever been near. Couldn't stop shivering. 'What the Naid did I do that was so bad, huh? They *really* disapprove of beer, huh? Or little bars? Or watching The Game?'

***

I dunno what started them jumping all over me that night in the bar at the Plough. Nor why they changed again, just as fast, after twenty-odd days in the sluice. I suppose it was their idea of being nice to me. Suddenly got me cleaned up, medicked and patched. Rigged me up to tubes and wires when I refused to eat and drink.

S'funny – you can taste the oranssa even through a dripline. Strapped me down again.

A different one – young, I think, and male, judging from the facial colour and the ID badge – came in while I was held down helpless – as so often. He stood over me for a minin and I thought he was going to lacerate me or something in temper. Kinda nothing you can do in a situation like that. Except wait and try not to shriek and scream too soon. He looked me up and down like I was a poor specimen on his bench – which I probably had been a few times.

But he pulled a chair closer and sat next to me. 'You need the oranssa, Prisoner Honi… Alika. Some of the ferols, and the sterol proteins in our diet would be too high for you. You also require trace amounts of other ingredients. You're a total imbalance from the looks of the chart here. You wouldn't survive well on a diet too much like ours. Not without this supplement – it'll remove some of the excess traces.'

He studied the screen that he brought up. 'Drunk some beer, have you? Hmm… this should counteract a couple of the ingredients in that… and you seem to need a much greater range of the enzymal acids than we do – across the whole thio- and ascorbic-acid vitamin spectrum. Maybe you're more closely related to the Lintuja than us. Ninety percent similar, though.'

Sure he sounded genuine, but who knows with them? Could just as easily have been their usual dollop of deceit.

'Think about how willing you are to cooperate. But, whatever you choose, you will have the oranssa every day.' He waited for my response, but I was still pondering and cursing when he rose, and left.

‘You *shall* do as we say.’ It was Van Kalin come back. Probably in disgrace for loosening my leash round the nightlife of the compound. She didn’t say anything about the whole episode. I asked, but she was silent – not a word or a click. And I don’t read their faces well enough to pick up any feelings.

She slackened the strapping off me. ‘Decide soon,’ she said, and she slid out when I didn’t answer her, either.

Another different one brought things in. Showed me how they worked – screens and electro-tools; some things like old books and scribing paps; and left me with a communi-screen. But Jeeps it was so boring. I piped into three local channels, picked up the local vernacular from something like NorthGutters that over-dramatized everything from a nuclear war to a sniffle and cursed and clouted each other ten times per episode.

I guess it rubbed off on me – I had no interest in such drivel, but the total normality and banality was so Terruusan. I was still thoroughly pissed. Locked in a twelve by twelve. Missing MAzzy and JUddy and Terruusi and the Base guys. Nothing to do except fend the Mikita off – except they didn’t do much with me most of the time. But I was learning about them. My last order, ‘Stay there’, must have been so I would learn about them. I will learn – the whole point of remaining – to study them.

One came in when I was writing and drawing something about a space-guy I once knew who’d got in a mess on some highly volcanic moon somewhere. I was only doing it to practise my written language – and I liked drawing when I was a kid. And this Miki just stalked in. After I'd told Van Kilan it was polite to knock as you entered. Deliberate ignorance, barging in, all teeth and tail swish and I just lost it and threw the set at him, and the tools case and the things I'd been working on, and smashed the viestinta set. 'Treat me like droppings, and I'll act like'em.' I ranted at him, and we were gong at each other, fist to claw.

Tough little lizzies, they are. But I imagine they had to carry him out, when they'd all given me a thorough stomping and narco'd me. That was it. They left me again. *I'm still at Square One.* No food or anything for Naid-alone knows how long – days, anyway. Leg going rotten with something yellowy-blue. Maybe they expected me to learn something from it. I didn't, except maybe – Get as much smashing up done as you can before they jump on you.

Four days this time, before Van Kalin came visiting, torn between ordering me about and placating me – then sniffing and ripping at my clothes and doing a frilly-wobble – she was straight on her viestinta for help, and panicking. They all came in. Yucking and oogling at my leg. I'd been thinking the blood was getting poisoned enough to kill me and fool them all. They got it, too. Yippering at me – cross and concerned. *Should damn treat me better*, I thought as I passed out again. I did a lot of that when they weren't happy. Peaceful, it was. Except for some really shit and weird dreams.

Someone must have relented. Still got my leg, Naid-alone knows how long after. Still here. But back in my "apartment" – single-room-but-more-space-than-a-cell. Kalin came and talked at me a lot and I wouldn't talk much back. Not at first. Till she was getting the idea that I was more than a mite pissed about it all. 'Dunno why you stopped letting me go out at night… I was okay, not going anywhere – hardly could, could I? I'd scarcely merge in, huh?'

Still she wouldn't say why they'd let me out all them nights, or why they'd stopped it so suddenly. The flag dropped – 'Different factions among you, eh?' I said. 'Bit of infighting? Who's winning?'

Not her, by the look on her face. Really distinct something – embarrassment. Maybe. Not comfortable, anyway.

So I carried on, 'Who's pushing the keys this decc, eh, if not you Research bunch? The military? Politicos? Locals? Off-World Department?'

I was right with one of them, 'Great, I'm a shuttleball, am I? And the other team's got me? I wanna be dead,' I told her. 'Just not exist any longer. My MAzzy must have been told I died… how long ago now? Three years?'

'Five,' she said.

'Five years a prisoner?' *Not a word of the conflict, relations, other prisoners.* 'You treat me like dung, ignore me… threaten me… clout and stomp me.' I stopped asking or trying to find out anything ages ago. Then I stopped wondering. Too busy hanging on to life, surviving, keeping sane. Until now. Now I don't care. *MAzzy wouldn't want me returning now. She must have someone new…* I was ranting it to myself as much as Van Kalin… trying to keep it inside… *Has MAzzy taken up with some guy I knew? Friend? Someone from Main Base? The captain who ordered me to stay? Or back home on Terruus? Shut it Alik. Don't torment yourself. Say no more… just die. No – Got to stop here*

– *orders were to stay.* I know I was sobbing. Hating everything, especially me. 'I should have had the guts to kill myself first chance I had… but there'd been hope back then. Now, Kalin… I got *nothing.'*

She gave me the hard, inscrutable look. Cold eyes, they have, near black. Can't read'em.

'Nobody's winning. But there has been a change.' She was being weighty with her delivery, 'You have this *huoneisto* again, your apartment. You may return to the level you attained before… *before.'*

I couldn't tell if she was stating facts, making an offer, or issuing a challenge.

Seated on the edge of the bed, I took it as an offer rather than an ultimatum… *Got to decide myself, hmm?* Naid. I was torn up. *'I can't. Not again. It's too…'*

'Honi.' She was hesitant. 'Alika… There are different views and directions. About you. About other things. Priorities change. Circumstances alter. Sometimes one matters, and at other times not.' She left the door open when she left, 'You know where the lounge is… and the canteen… and the rest.'

It took me half an hour sitting there to decide, *One more chance, then I'm off the roof if they naid me up again.*

***

The bars hadn't changed. One caff-diner was always busy with non-military lizzies and visitors, including some birdies – the Lintuja. Hard to decide on them – they seemed to be less intense than their allies… acted like they were higher status, too. Or rank. Talking with them was hard work at first, but I didn't talk military or politics, so they were okay. Food, drink and various team games they enjoyed joking about.

Laughing a lot – and they have really weird laughs – they invited me to The Game that evening. Not Kynsi, like I expected. I think it was a bit like riccku, with an even weirder off-hide rule than vaccball. They tried to explain it to me, and to some of their own members, too. But we had a great time. Cheering for Naid-alone knows who or what and I didn't get back to my *huoneisto* until mid-morning next day

Not long afterwards, I had a sort of little job, meeting and greeting Litty tourists, and taking them to whatever game was in town that night. It meant learning a lot about the rules and tactics, though understanding them was a challenge. But I was almost excited at the thought of actually doing something – tourist escort! Like wow, huh?

The food had become almost edible; a mix of canteen and a couple of bars and the caff-diner. No – that's disingenuous of me – In truth, I like their food fare. Some terrific spices they have; and the *rakka* pies are awesome to my uncultured palate. There's a special beer they have, too. I always have to start the evening with an oranssa, though, and log it in. Just checking on what the young one had told me that day, I asked about it when a fresh container was delivered one day. 'As I understand it,' the delivery guy said, 'it's to keep you topped up on vitamins and minerals; proteins and stuff, that aren't generally in the food we eat. And your metabolism needs them. Something like that.' He even managed a recognisable shrug.

Two smart civilian Mikita who I chatted with in a bar wanted to talk about anything and everything to do with home and people and interests. I didn't feel like I was giving any Fed secrets away, and I didn't get any impression that they were doing it for any ulterior purpose. Yes, I know – totally naïve. I wondered if I'd been got at? Had they mixed my mind? I never felt evangelical for or against the Mikita or Lintuja; or against home – My wife was there... friends... comrades.

I asked them why they wanted to know.

'We wish to learn about Terran Federation,' they said. 'And to speak some of their words. *Your* words.' One of them reminded me of MAzzy – something about her way of re-questioning with a lilt in her voice and tilt of her head. I missed MAzzy so much; and JUddy. No news of any kind about anything. *I'm still on the same planet – Koti means "Home". That's important: it hasn't been invaded or destroyed by TerraFed. So maybe the Mikita are still expanding their colonising; or there'd been a standoff? Consolidating?*

These two knew a lot about everything, it seemed, and told me some things, and showed me a couple of reports, but they were about places I never heard of. And I was just feeling so homesick for Terruusi, for MAzzy, for speaking in straight Stang, not parrot Miki – No, that's me being untruthful again – I'm fairly fluent in Miki now, and medium in Lintuja – plus Terri and Stang, of course, but I haven't spoken casual Terri for years – except to myself, cos I think in it. And I talk aloud to myself in Terri and Stang a lot, with lashings of curses, colloquials and vernaculars in case they're recording me and trying to analyse what I say. They'd struggle with the foul-mouthed metaphoric mess that I come out with: it don't make much sense to me most of the time.

I'm getting desperate for human company – for a relaxed chat, a smile, some warmth of a shared past, heritage. I haven't seen or spoken with another human for… six? Years. What's that imply – no other prisoners? Is there a war, skirmishes, or friction-free expansion around each other, or what? Has Humanity lost? Been driven away from this region? Whichever, I've sure been crossed off, forgotten.

The Mikita? I dunno. I don't *like* them, as such. I fear them too much to like them: they have total power over me. They could do anything at the turn of a card. I could be executed, brain-wiped, put back in the Square. I spent my first two years there. I crave for home, friends, my own language instead of these non-human lizzies and birdies. Sure, I understand them, but they're not given to home-tongue casual, informal, natural chatter.

***

I was called into The Block. Some over-dressed Miki officer told me that my return had been mentioned in a meeting, as an aside to something important.

'Return?' I was frightened at the thought. 'To The Block? That cell?'

'No. Return,' he said again.

'Where to? TerraFed?' *What would I be? A misfit? I was ordered to remain. Not allowed to go home. After all this time here, getting accustomed to them, I'd be so scared to face TerraFed people… Terruusi. Have they brained me with some compulsion to remain here? Or my own people? – The last thing they said was, 'Stay there.' I had to remain at my post; hold my position. That's drilled into me.*

'I can leave? Why now? What's going on? Are you serious?'

The decorated officer knew little; he couldn't or wouldn't answer anything. Some things, he definitely knew, and others, he was in the dark over. 'Simply a remark, that it had been mentioned higher up. Part of something else. But, yes, it has been, er, mooted, that you might be returned to the Terran Federation.'

Naida! What do I do? So sudden... 'What's happening out there? When?' I asked.

He shrugged a neck frill, 'No date was mentioned, Prisoner Honi. But, I wouldn't have called you in unless it was a definite possibility. You should prepare yourself.'

Would Terra lock me away? I was told to stay. Not trust me ever again? 'Is this a prisoner exchange programme? Am I an example of your fair treatment of captives? A witness to your civilisation, and your non-evil?'

He shrugged again, looking impatient with me.

Or has TerraFed found I'm here, and want me back? Fat chance; they'll be so suspicious of me – that I'm turned, booby-trapped or something like that.

But, I really do want to go back. Be with JUddy, MAzzy... At least see them again, even if MAzzy's with someone else...

***

Just today, I heard that someone higher up had sanctioned the proposal that I'm to be released, to go home – as an ambassador. There's an agreement being worked out over whole-region policies, centred on Koti, and they want someone to accompany the official group as a kind of go-between, or liaison.

I was called in. Four of them were there – Van Kilan and the Deco Officer, a Lintuja, and a non-uniform Miki female who had a very smart turn of neck frill. 'We have no agenda for you. Merely to be there, to be consulted, or used as your Federation people see fit. To answer questions, whatever. Tell them if you think our people are being devious, lying. Be honest.'

'And it's imminent,' the Deco Officer said.

***

I was part of the delegation that left Koti to a fanfare of trimpiti and ksilofonlar. I suppose I was treated like one of the others, the Mikita and the Lintuja, and was one of the general mix of the party all the time we travelled. The same when we were disembarking at Neutraalia for the big peace conference and talks. The TerraFed people knew I was accompanying the delegation; they must have my history. And would surely have informed MAzzy? *Hugely momentous, this. My heart was fluttering, racing, my blood up... Six years! Free again. Free as a military underling ever is.*

But I wasn't greeted any differently to the others. No big welcome. Nothing. No sign of MAzzy. 'Must be keeping their heads down, watching me, sizing me up. Awaiting their opportunity to speak with me, debrief me, get all the back-story info on the Mikita, I expect.

My first sight of humans! I could scarcely speak for staring – free, chattering humans the other side of the room. Hearing their voices, seeing their expressions, feeling their warmth…

***

Even after a full day, and two nights, it's still not working out too well. It's as if they don't trust me. Can't blame them, I suppose, after all this time. I really expected someone to contact me at the termination of the first meeting, to take me away, welcome me back. *Anything*. But I spent the day with the delegation from Koti, feeling like a stranger among my own people. And another night without MAzzy and JUddy.

Then, on my way to the breakfast salon – I was looking forward to an oranssa-free meal – two TerraFed officials in Conference uniforms joined me, kept in step either side of me, and guided me through huge bronze-bound doors, and down a wide corridor.

'Where are we going? Who are you? Who am I to see? Is my wife here?'

'All in due course,' they told me. 'there's another matter first.'

Naid! I bet they mean me disobeying orders to stay on Calinkyor, at Koti. Sure as Sherrif a'Beth, they led me to a room where they could speak with me.

Except… I'm back in a Square One room, imprisoned by my fellow humans. I've been here for hours. I'm alone. They must be watching me through the mirror-blank windows. I wonder if MAzzy is through there? I go close to the mirror window and try to look through, 'MAzzy? Are you there?'

I really don't think my thoughts and beliefs have changed. I can't have aged so much that they don't recognise me. Studying myself in the mirrors, I don't look particularly different, even after nearly seven years with the Mikita. I've not changed: my scales have always had exactly that rather-fetching orange sheen. Okay, my neck frill is a touch longer than it once was, but that's to be expected. My eyes are the same sparkling midnight that MAzzy always said she loved, and my teeth are beautifully sharp. I cannot imagine what they're scared of. I flick my tail in anticipation – it'll be really good to see MAzzy and JUddy again.

TRAFFIC

This is terrible. I'll miss my ship home. Why does this stupid bridge have to be shut again? Or shit again, as the humans say. 'Clifton Bridge has been a load of crap since they opened the damn thing.' I hear it every fruggling day.

They say it created the traffic over the River Trent when it was built; and these days it's stopping it. Rusting reinforcement bars in the concrete supports now, they reckon. Could collapse, or drop sections onto vehicles passing under the bridge. Okay, but who cares about a few flat cars? Or why don't they just close the underpass and leave the main road across the bridge open? But no – they always think they've got to over-react so it looks like they care, or are earning their grubby money by looking like they're doing something. Humans! I despair of these Earthies sometimes, especially when I'm stuck in their endless queues of vehicles going nowhere.

All very well for the rest of them stuck in this queue, but I bet they don't have a spaceship taking off any minute. I look like missing my trip home because of some old iron bars going rusty inside the concrete of an eyesore of a bridge.

So, today of all days, I'm stuck in the worst fruggling traffic ever. Four-lane carriageway being shunted down to one so we can crawl across a useless falling-to-bits bridge. I've been on this frantic dump of a planet for half a year. That's a half-year too long.

Ahh! Movement.

Jerking forward—

Shuggery! Some tatty little Audi chopped me up.

BMW trying to force in – he's got no chance.

Two asswipes in front almost hit each other.

Brake hard—

Oops – Nearly banged my tendrils on the windscreen. I do a quick check that anybody in the outside world is still seeing the human mock-up version of me projected onto the windows. World? Huh. Not much of one. Especially when they do this kind of thing to me.

Fruggles! Nothing's moving ahead. I *need* to move. Come on. Come on. Solid vehicles all round, like being drowned in a metal sea – like on Logjam.

Ah! If I'm careful, I can light-hop ahead and they'll never notice. Right… eyes everywhere for an opportunity – not difficult when they're on the tip of every tendril. Okay… If I sub-vap that one, I can hop ahead into his spot. He'll never notice. Anybody else might be blinking and not notice. Most of'em on the roads are kaylied this time of day, anyway, coming south out of Nottingham.

Oh, yes! Done it. Easy. Nicely done, if I do say so myself. With four mouths – two reserved for speaking – it's easy to say it myself.

And again… Yes! Great. This is better. Nobody leaning on their horns. Fat load of good it would do them if they did.

Come on… come on. Get this traffic on the move. It's so *slow*. I *need* to get there. My ship'll be taking off soon. It won't wait. Can't wait. I'll be stuck here for another half-year – over two thousand of their years. I really can't face any longer on this dreadful planet. Fruggles, this is getting desperate.

Again… Ah, yes. This is progress – getting closer to the bridge now. Try a couple of places ahead next time – I'm getting good at the timing. But. I need to be in the other lane. So, I'm all eyes – and tendrils – for another chance. Signal so they know. Wait… Yes. *Now*. Vanish that one, and shift over.

Fruggle-it! Where'd *he* come from? Silent and fast up the inside, little white van man leapt into the space I just created – It was *my* damn space! I made it. For *me*. So he's got to go. Treating me like that! Acting like all the other drivers are aliens who don't matter. So I vapped him – Zappp! Gone – and straight re-formed into his place. Like I told the dash-recorder, 'He's probably in orbit round Yunrid by now.' No loss.

Chuff, chuff! I could fly faster than this – except my wings are triple-folded when I'm driving, and it takes five minutes to unfurl, inflate, and get a full head of haemoid pumping through them. All while I'm on display outside. So that's not on.

Ahh. Traffic moving ahead. I can see progress a hundred metres in front, where it's one lane. So it should be starting to move a bit steadier. Might make it yet.

Oh, ay up, what's this bollard-brain up to? Some ranting lunatic behind me is out his car and coming this way. Here he comes… Raving at me. He noticed something, I expect. Smacking his hand on my side-window. All he'll be seeing will be my human hologram looking steadfastly at the road ahead. But he's irate, sure enough, so I have the choice of vapping him, or winding down.

The vapping was tempting, but I restrained myself, and wound my window down, and gave him *The Glare* – massed tendrils and eyes, plus ears like cabbage leaves, all waving at him.

I imagine he'll be in hospital some time, the apoplexy he had when he saw the real me sitting here. It wasn't helped by staggering away, falling over the barrier backwards and landing, I presume, on the carriageway below. It slowed the traffic down behind me, too, with his car just sitting there blocking them. But I merely wrapped my tentacles back inside, sucked my globulatory organs into place, and eased forward as there was a sudden space ahead. I'd have climbed out to have a look, but I don't do caring. Not about Earthies, anyway.

Besides, if I get out this vehicle, I'll just have to spread my wings – they're feeling really confined and stiff after all this time in here.

And I really don't want to do a full stretch in public again. Fruggle!

Look at all the fuss it caused that last time, when I was new here! Oh, my tainted tendrils! The humans are still going on about it – even after two thousand years they don't let you forget… still making a big deal out of it.

I go purple to think back then, when we'd been stuck for *so* long, and we sheltered in this out-the-way hovel for the night. I was getting terrible cramps in my pecs and lats and I just had to flex my feathery bits – you know, spread my wings, get the juices flowing.

We didn't think there were any humans in there with us. But, of course, these Earthies – they got it all round their necks – totally wrong impression about me. Don't know what they thought I was.

I swore that would be the last time I ever stretched my wings in public, or took refuge in a fruggling stable, especially in anywhere called Bethlehem.

WE JUST RUFFLED THEM UP

'Come on, Alqy, we just ruffled them up a little. Nothing. It was a joke. They shouldn'a been here. It's Guyzard territory – ours.' Lazing back, Malkoth was confident there was no comeback on a mere playtime incident. He waved a very impressive pincer to reinforce the message that he wasn't troubled in the least.

'No – it's officially human territory. Their sphere of influence. We're the guests here.' Ambassador Alquin was supremely patient. Perseverance was one of many qualities he needed in his role as liaison, arbitrator, smoother and maintainer of discipline among his people, the Guyzards, especially the ones who thought they were above the law, such as this party.

'Aw… Come on, Ambassador, we took the region over. It's been ours for yonkeys' years. Besides, they were disturbing us.' Malkoth grindled around his small party of friends and fellow hunters.

'How were they disturbing you?' The ambassador had a sinking feeling in his thoracic cavity.

'By… by existing. By coming here. Holding their own party – big posh affair.'

'In the place where you were already partying?' Alquin had to be sure of all the circumstances and justifications.

'Sure, fishing; you know, hunting.'

'Hunting?'

‘Sure. Local wildlife. You know, vacation time, out on The Fringes. They get the shemmins coming through; and woliffs; the occasional grizzled ursa. Plus maybe a human or two. What are we supposed to do?’

‘Welcome them? Stand aside. Move well clear? It’s *their* land, Malkoth. You could let them pass in peace and hope they don’t take umbrage at your illicit presence? Bow?’

‘Bow!? To a human? They’re nothing. Dirt.’ Karamith joined in, his extra-long fringe palps showing above the rest of Malkoth’s group. The others grindled in agreement. Shuffling in smug superiority at the ambassador.

‘It’s *their* territory,’ Alquin insisted. ‘Officially, and in fact and practise. You should *not* have done it.’

‘What? Playing with a shipload of human interlopers is disapproved of now, is it? We just ruffled them up a little. Nothing.’ Malkoth dismissed the whole idea of criticism of his actions.

‘For Choglog’s sake, Malkoth. How many more times? *It’s human territory.* We’re the guests. You any idea who you killed? Even how many?’

‘Who cares?’ Malkoth’s companions were nodding and agreeing with every word he spoke.

‘*You* will. What the flug did you do to them?’ He bristled in impotent anger at the unlistening fool before him.

‘Pulled a few apart. You know… arms, legs… anything else that stuck out.’ He giffled. ‘Got a couple of heads in the back of my Ess-Yoot. Look just fine there.’

‘Not on a trophy rack?’ The ambassador was in sub-kirric shock. ‘Tell me you haven’t? I shall have to report this.’

‘Think that’ll do you any good, Alqy? But if you do, there’ll be bother for you. Just remember who my father is.’

‘There’ll be bother for us all if I don’t.’

‘Ah, you again, Ambassador.’ Malkoth didn’t bother to stand. ‘What news this time? A few more humans for us to spit-roast this time?’

Alquin’s stomach churned at the thought of the next half-hour, especially after the dressing down he’d had for reporting Malkoth in the first place. *What it is to move in high circles – and to have friends in higher ones. But, with fortune, I’ll get through it and it will all be smoothed over.* ‘It turns out the party you, er, “ruffled up a bit”, was the human delegation to Station 1, gathering together at their summer vacation villa before moving on for the Peace and Concessions Conference.’

Malkoth shrugged. ‘So what? Plenty more of them. Who wants peace with pasty squishy little things like them, anyway?’

This isn’t going to be easy. But, I must do something. ‘I am expected to hand you over to the human community at Farmland Four,’ he said, slightly nervously, in view of Malkoth’s status and pincer-size. ‘I understand that there are severe penalties for killing humans, or anything else that’s sentient, apparently.’

He gazed at the lounging group of erstwhile party-makers who had caused him so much sleeplessness of late. *I'm actually expected to execute you all, within the day. But a handover would let the humans do it in their own way, and I'd be in the clear.*

'I must ask you once more to save an awful lot of trouble, and go to the humans and confess—'

'Severe penalties? For me? No such thing, Alquin. You do recall who my clone-father is, don't you? There'll be no comeback on me – I told you that before.'

'Well…' Ambassador Alquin shuffled on all six main legs, and his stabiliser legs, too. 'I have been in contact with the human liaison office, and have tried to stall any action they might consider taking. I continue to invent problems with the process, and hope that time will heal, and something else will divert their ongoing insistence.'

'Good for you, Alquin – it's your job. Now push off, hmm? You're blocking my view.' Malkoth grindled round his sycophants and they all raised a defiant drink in the direction of the ambassador.

'You idiots!' The ambassador railed, 'You must hand yourselves in to the humans – this is their territory. If you tell them your status, and ask for mercy—'

'How long have we been hiring imbeciles for ambassadors? Nobody's handing anyone anywhere—'

'You *must*. They have let it be known that a great deal depends on this. On principal. They've let it be known that they are prepared to make this a very wide-ranging matter. Very extensive repercussions, they'd intimated. So you need to go to them, and admit it all, and ensure that any repercussions are limited to just you few.'

‘Your entertainment value is wonderful, Alqy; but you’re zero in sense.’

‘Er… the humans have threatened to take strong, widespread retaliatory action themselves if we are not forthcoming—'

‘Forthcoming? You mean handing me over to them?’

‘Not only you. All of you. The whole party group, for trial and justice.’

‘The only justice they’ll get is in the jaws of a pincer – again.’ He chortled as no other Guyzard could.

But Ambassador Alquin was persistent, if not overly courageous in his decisions and requests. *If I push this too much, he’ll get me the sack. Can’t be having that. I could send my Full-Squad in and get it done. But where would that leave me?* ‘They know you dismembered their people. It was High Lady Hassandra and her retinue. Thirteen of them from the highest levels of human society and government.’

Malkoth sniggered and allowed a servant to slip another drink into his fore-grip.

‘The Peace Accord is at threat, Malkoth. They say that, to convince us, they will teach us what it is like to be dismembered, alive. On a mass scale, they said. And I think they mean that very literally. It really might be better for all our people on this planet if you could see your way to at least going to Farmland Four to explain, and apologise.’

‘Huh, as if. Apologise? For de-boning a few humans? Like how are they thinking of dismembering us? We’re the ones with razor pincers, not them.’ To emphasise his point, Malkoth slid his guard sheath off his main right pincer. He liked to wave it gently – more magnificent than anyone else’s there.

‘The humans warned that they have developed strong psycho-kinaesthesic chemicals and procedures.’

‘Sure they have.’ Karamith butted in. ‘We going to inject ourselves with stuff so we follow their orders? Surrender? Hand ourselves over?’

‘Just for ruffling up a few squidgy little humans?’ Malkoth could be so arrogantly dismissive.

‘It’s never going to happen – the humans can go eviscerate themselves.’ Kolgart was coming closer, clearly beginning to get worked up about this afront to the social standing, and actual physical threats. ‘Huh – from *humans?’*

‘They gonna persuade us to take pills, so we obey them?’ It was Karamith’s turn to grindle around the group.

‘They got secret rays from satellites beaming over us, making us think their way? Do what they want?’ Malkoth slid the guard sheath off his main pincer left as well.

Not to be intimidated by such a show, Alquin exposed his main right pincer as well, secure in the knowledge that it was equally as formidable as Malkoth’s. *Or any of them,* he gazed round the group, knowing that, when it came down to the squeeze, he would defy the human diktat, and side, as always, with his own people first, last and every time. *It’s the way of the Guyzards.*

‘Are they going to knock us all out and start cutting pieces off us?’ Karamith wanted to know, strutting in small, impatient circles.

‘What? Crack a few shells?’ The thought of a horde of soft little humans doing anything to the mighty

Guyzards was clearly ludicrous, even to Ambassador Alquin.

'What?' One of Kolgart's companions called. 'Are they going to tie us down one at a time so they can pull alternate legs off? Or – horror – of horrors – remove the top section of a main right pincer?' He shuddered at the thought – almost delicious in its dreadfulness.

'We don't know what kind of technologies the humans have – perhaps something they might release into the air?'

'Sure… and knock us out; carry us away?'

'Ain't going to happen, Alquin. We're much too big and powerful to have to listen to what they want.'

'And too many of us.' The whole party group was joining in the rebelliousness. Even Ambassador Alquin was becoming caught up in the mood of defiance.

'There are accords in place.'

'Which we – you – have broken.'

'Well, what did they expect? Coming through while we were in party mood.'

The Ambassador noticed that a couple of the others in the group had removed their main shields as well. And, just entering, four of his own people already didn't have pincer-guards in place.

'You smell something?'

They all sniffed, looked round, pincers gleaming sharply. 'What? Something in the air? No…' But they were eyeing each other warily, a pincer or two clicking in anticipation of the midday meal.

Alquin sniffed the air again, clicked his pincers a couple of times in sudden hunger. *I could rather fancy something to eat... Malkoth, perhaps.'*

Firming to the idea, he focused on the thought of early luncheon, and launched himself at Malkoth, aware that many others had equally abruptly attacked a neighbour, clearly intent on ripping them apart.

Ahh, he thought with a flash of insight, *I see how the humans might make it work,* as he crunched down on Malkoth's abdomen, suddenly aware of screamingly terrible, agonising pain in his own thorax as he dedicatedly dined on the shrieking, hissing flesh of the cause of all his recent worries. *Extremely wide-ranging retaliation, they'd threatened.*

WEEDING

'I've got some weeding to do down the far end, Esprita. I'll potter round a bit while I'm over there, bit of tidying up I've been meaning to get round to. I'll be back in time for Tiffin's Sunset.'

'I thought it was mostly looking fine, dear. Very neat, actually.'

'Hmm?' Tuan Roh swirled his orbit a few times, and set a few dwarf planets spinning ultra-fast, just for an idle twist of the mind. 'It mostly is, of course, but I noticed some time ago that it was becoming a little overgrown on the far fringes; overspreading the bounds out towards the Orpal Wisp. It merely requires snipping back here and there.'

'Don't go too mad, dear. A little judicious pruning works wonders, and saves that awful dead look those Berkerut planets had for so long. I was almost embarrassed to go that way to the Supernova Celebration last year.'

'Alright, I won't do that again – I did learn from that experience, I promise.'

'Good. Have a relaxing time, dear, and don't forget that all the little creeperties need *somewhere* to live.'

'Not in my lot, they don't.' Tuan Roh was very conscious of his position as total master of this star cluster, the Tuan's Ring – with the dense dust cloud in its centre, giving the appearance of hollowness. He felt it was his duty to keep it as his forebears would have done. *But as Esprita says, times change things – some new star material drifting in... a little heating up in the overall background figure... I'll have to make plans for that aspect before long. Even a nova, not long after I first took on the responsibility.* He felt a little responsible for that, knowing he could have forestalled it, 'But I'd never seen a nova before, and on my own property, too. Good experience for a novice, like I was.'

'Oh, come on, dear,' Esprita wasn't going to unleash me without her dire-warning tone of voice, 'the miniscules don't look particularly untidy down there. Not harming anyone... and not an eyesore to passers-by, either.'

'I don't like stuff growing where I didn't plant it, dear. It goes against my grand scheme.'

You don't have a scheme, dear, grand or otherwise; merely an idea when we began here – a whimsical thought. Promise me you won't leave any of those little worlds all barren and bare again, hmm? *Like the Berkeruts.'*

'Yes, yes, I know. You'll not let me forget that, will you? I promise.' He still nursed a bruised ego and cheyla from her sulking chastisement on that occasion; and no wraithing and writhing for three solar yonks, either.

Sighing deeply, they exchanged sarilmaks and he was gone, 'Nothing too rash, dear,' she ultra-thought after him.

Tightening his cayon and his resolve, Tuan Roh meandered proudly among the 180 well controlled and cultivated planets throughout his cluster, each one a source of pleasure and vanity – which he admitted to most readily. *They're so precisely how I want them, expect them to be.*

Reaching the further, marginal area of his planet-strewn plot, he turned his attention to the 27 wilder planets of the fringe region, where Orpal's scattered untidy Wisp of stars began. Distractedly, he pulled a sirifica in disapproval at the idea of allowing planetary creeperties to run loose – *So much not a credit to me,* he wrinkled his wraiths in faint loathing. *I'd better get among the neglected tri-nine, I suppose.* Decided, he swished silently in the direction of the nearest one. In passing, he tugged a wandering cometary swarm back on a tighter orbit, and straightened up a planetary wobble that was beginning to correct itself, anyway.

Maybe Esprita's right – I'm getting too fussy. Perhaps I should branch out a little in a new direction. Not a wildlife cluster, never. The thought was shudderingly awful, and the idea faded when he began to dissipate himself around, 'Oh by the Lords of Creation! Some of these planets are just expanding their creeping populations far beyond the limits. I can *not* be having that. They're utterly out of control. I shouldn't have neglected them for so long. Oh, yes indeed, there's a need to dig out these unruly planets. I've allowed them too much freedom – well out of control. Whatever Esprita says, all these life forms are just too much for a tidy garden, even along the borders. They need rooting out. Oh, dear – especially *these* horrible things – they'll have to go…'

He tugged and viperated at a range of life forms that he didn't like the look of. *I'll only eradicate the mobile forms, not the green, static ones – don't want Esprita to find I've completely cleared all life-forms from the planets again. And if I empty a few where these things have spread to. Vile weed creeperties,* he huffed inwardly and exhaled, entirely sterilising a particularly overgrown planet with some especially weird creepies.

Let's have a look at Zodron. *Urghh. Got to go.*

Yupitra? *I'll merely pull a few of the most aggressive creepies out.*

Herosthese? *A good wipe-down should do... yesss... Nicely done.*

Aluma? *Oh dear, can't leave that – they're spreading everywhere. So invasive; neighbouring planets being taken over and swamped. Dear, dear, dear, no. They've got to go.*

Pausing at the end of a tract, he swirled back to admire his wraithiwork. *So clean – Hmm, perhaps I shouldn't have cleaned out all the indigenous mobile creeperty populations quite so thoroughly. Esprita'll have another favour-withdrawing episode. But, really, they shouldn't have been so spready.*

Perhaps if I said it was to make better room for one of the others, one with nicer creeperties; not all these sub-mecho and sectoid things. Let's have a look among these other planets and see if there are some more *surfacey* little crawlies. No point having underground wormy things... Mmm, have something we all see from above. Oops – I'd better get a bit of a swirl on, Esprita'll be expecting me back for Sunset on Tiffins.

How about that one? Mmm... well, it's a bubbling little planet. Quite pretty in its own variegated way. It can't be too bad if they've still got mixed environs, no scorched-off regions. And still stuck on their own mudball without mass inter-creeperty slaughter. Let's have an insta-squint at them... Hmm, not keen on *that.*

Nor *that*. They've done well there, though. Oh, well. If I leave them to spread out, they'll reach the other planets before long, the ones I just vacated. I'll tell Esprita I cleared them especially for this lot to expand into.

Let's have a last look for now… So many of them packed on there, it's amazing they're not at war all the time. And still haven't discovered any of the eight interstellar steps. Amazing they haven't destroyed themselves already. Must have something going for them.

He turned to go. Tiffins Sunset doesn't wait, unless I *want* to upset all the others, I suppose. A wickedinceous smile played fleetingly across his esternales.

Or perhaps I should give them a nudge – so Esprita can see some clear progress before she "happens" to be visiting in this direction. I could speed them up a mite. Mmm, yes… I could spread a little mental fertiliser, perhaps…

There, done. Now, Serith to Gerith, I must dash…

Corinne Sanchez (Mz) looked up from her desk in the research library at Boston's prestigious NASA-supporting Ion Drive Research Centre. Cocking her head on one side, *It seems so clear now. Yes...* She cocked her head the other way, to follow the train of thought. *Yes, yes... that would work. And if we... Ah. Indeed, yes. Then it would need...* A blank Word page, fingers racing and jabbing, trying to keep up with the thoughts that burst and splurted and washed through her. The CID, she keyed in – The Corinne Ion Drive. Fingers speeding and juggling, paper pad by her hand for swift diagrammatic notes. Her eyes danced with her fingers. *This is it! This is it!* For an age, she shook away offers of drink, to come for a snack, to give it a rest. What you doing? What's all that mean?

'Security's locking you in, Corinne. You got a key?' She didn't hear them.

By dawn she'd slept at the console for two one-hour snatches, had four painkillers for RSI and had a raging thirst for tequila and bitters. And a completed treatise, multiply copied and password-protected. She sighed and stretched, 'It's time to go see Prof. We're meeting the NASA Power-Unit Team this p.m. And Shit! Have we got something to show them.'

**

Albert Zryj, fascinated as always with the puzzles of ultra-light-speed waves in his laboratory at the Warsaw Sciendo Instytut, stopped and checked the formula. *That's where I've been going wrong. If I... Yes, a tweak there should... Dobry panie! It works!*

**

Sanshreya Paret looked one more time at the astro-time algorithm. *How did I not see that discrepancy before...? This could be The Answer... If Time in a relative Time-vacuum could be induced to bend... thus...*

**

Pete Hawks stared into the white heat of the crucible. It was destined to be part of a Rolls Royce engine – the experimental – aren't they all? – V9 H4. *But if we varied the percentage of... And if the edge curve was...* He grabbed a blank sheet from the work rota pad. 'Yes,

yes, yes! That's it! Gimme a biro!' he yelled, and began scribbling…

ABOUT THE AUTHOR

Trevor is a Nottinghamshire, UK writer. His short stories and poems have frequently won prizes, and he has appeared on television discussing local matters.

As well as SF short stories, he has published many reader-friendly books and articles, mostly about volcanoes around the world, and dinosaur footprints on Yorkshire's Jurassic coast.

He spent fourteen years at the classroom chalkface; sixteen as headteacher of a special school; and sixteen as an Ofsted school inspector to round it off. His teacher wife now jokes that it's "Sleeping with the Enemy".

In the 1980s, his Ph.D. research pioneered the use of computers in the education of children with profound learning difficulties.

Log on to https://www.sci-fi-author.com/

Amazon @ https://www.amazon.co.uk/~/e/B085GLPLKQ

Facebook @ https://www.facebook.com/graham.watts.545

BY THE SAME AUTHOR

OF OTHER TIMES AND SPACES

The Giant Anthology – 460 pages with 39 tales of here and now, and the futures that await us.

If you were spying on another planet, would you do any better than Dicky and Miriam in the snappy two-pager "Air Sacs and Frilly Bits".

Could you live among the laughs and lovers of "I'm a Squumaid"? Or cope with the heartache of "The Twelve Days of Crystal-Ammas"?

In the novella-length "The Colonist", how could anyone fault Davvy's actions in setting up Hill Six-Four-Six with a party of Highraff refugee women and children?

How might you cope in class with the all-knowing "Thank you, Mellissa" and her little yellow ducks? Would you be the guide for Reju Royalty when they insist on "Watching the Scurrugs"? Are we truly destined for the same fate that awaits this universe in "A Little Co-operation"?

According to eleven alien species and the author's mum, these are the brightest and most varied stories in the universe. With 19 illustrations and two poems to boost your orbit, this is Sci-Fi at its most original.

ZERO 9-4

Book 1 in the New-Classic Sci-Fi Series from the Lighter Side

Does Cleanup foretell the future of humanity? Or is it in the hands of the scientists who believe the key to space-time manipulation is Zero 9-4? Or is They Call the Wind Pariah a premonition of our fate in the grip of the Corona virus?

Are the aliens already among us in Betty? Or in the fire pit of Kalai Alaa? Or do they come on a Friday Night in Somercotes?

Dare you immerse yourself in the laughs and trials to come in It isn't easy being a Hero, or Holes aren't my Thing? Are you prepared to join the war of the alien genders in Kjid, or Typical Man?

These twenty-one tales from the lighter and darker sides, illuminated by fourteen quirky illustrations, are predicted to be voted the funniest and most thought-provoking in The Spiral Arm (the famous pub and restaurant on Ganymede) at the 2044 annual all-species barbecue.

ORBITAL SPAM

Book 2 in the New-Classic Sci-Fi Series from the Lighter Side

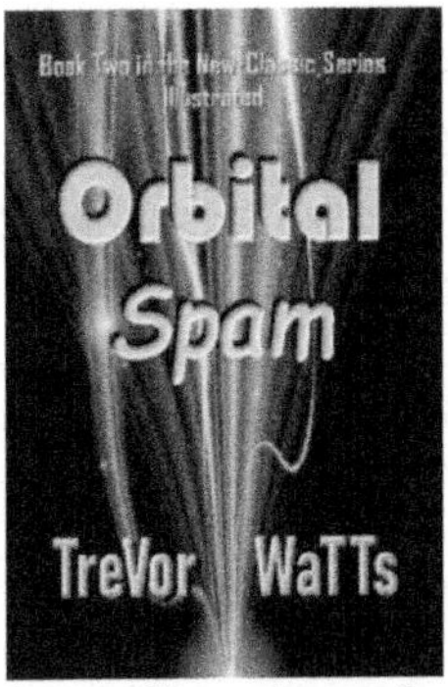

What would you do if you suspect your ship's been dumped in the Orbital Spam folder?

Is there anything you can you do when the Great Pondkeeper up in the sky decides to call time? Or when a trail of disembodied footprints heads straight for you across the wet concrete in Self-Levelling, how do you respond?

Would you answer the Prasap1 call?

From the laughs of To Somercotes and Beyond to the poignancy of What it Takes, these 20+ tales will alter your view of the future. The illustrations will brighten a boring wait at the space-port, or leisurely evening in orbit. Plus one poem: the beautiful, mysterious and stranded child – Mirador.

During his welcoming speech at the Xaatan Peace Conference, Duże Usta, the Galactic High Commissioner described this book as, "The most entertaining read I've had in seven millennia… a great step forward for humanity.

THE FRACTUS PROJECT

Book 4 in the New-Classic Sci-Fi Series from the Lighter Side

Is the human race condemned to remain extinct, or might a radical change to the Fractus Project bring them back?

Which of The New Colonists will the two elderly convict women choose, and what for?

Is this what you expected when you wrote the instructions that included the note Brackets Eradicated Close Brackets?

What would your decision be when the enemy ship comes Barrelling Towards Us?

As the Lumine Excessor elders brightly beamed at the Interstellar Sci-Fi Fair on Queens Orbit 7, "Laugh with them, cheer them on, or shed a lacrima, these stories are even more brilliant than us."

To be let of the leash in 2021. Check at www.sci-fi-author.com for details of timing and contents as they become known.

FURTHER YET

Book 5 in the New-Classic Sci-Fi Series from the Lighter Side

When you have a relationship with the friendly fruit in The Tangerine Affair, where's it all going to end?

Would you give up the secret of Vondur'Eye to the unseen interrogators of The Governa?

In Breach – Level 2, is the devastation amidships truly the end of the refugee colonists deep-frozen in the hold?

Terriff only has One Vote, but is he going to make it count when it comes to a decision about the Shinks?

Thrown out The Dome, with no idea why, how are you going to survive in the alien depths of the Agrantius Forest?

What is it that Effo the Maths Genius has forgotten?

Check for details of timing and contents at www.sci-fi-author.com

A FEW NOTES

These are all brand-new stories, except "Mansfield will never be the same again" and "I'm a Squumaid". These have been included in the introductory anthology, "Of Other Times and Spaces". The Squumaid story was one I particularly enjoyed writing, because, on its own, it developed a certain pace as I wrote and re-read it, becoming quite poetic. I long intended to re-write it in a more poetic form – and here it is.

Dear Maar'juh'rih was written for a book that was proposed by a writers' group in Nottingham, on the subject of letters. But it was the early months of Covid, and the project stalled. So you have first read of it.

Many of these stories had their origin in a real incident – such as the sudden closure of Clifton Bridge, in Nottingham on the day I was heading for the dentist. It was a mite desperate, but I made it. Thousands of other motorists have been delayed on a twice-daily basis ever since (to November 2020).

The cover story, "Terminal Space" was partly inspired simply by the picture itself. 'There must be a story there', I thought, and extended the beginnings of one that I'd begun some time before.

Similarly, I saw the picture of the girl's face for "The New Reality", and knew what that look meant. The story quickly grew.

"Polly" originally ended about ten lines earlier, but I read it out to a group and we talked about a better ending. Based on a jokey series of suggestions, I came up with this.

"A Higher Level"? I just love those little guys, as our American friends are wont to say.

"My Insensible Fingers"? Sometimes, a title just seems to be right.

The pictures are mostly adapted from the internet (where else, these days?) and are paid for, or are from one of the free sites which abound in the wifi world.

If you enjoy reading this book, please help me, and give it a positive review on Amazon – I really do appreciate it very much. If there's something you're not fond of, or that you wonder about, or want to say, ask on the blog at www.sci-fi.author.com

Many thanks for reading thus far, and May the 4th be with us (It's with my brother – it's his birthday).

Printed in Great Britain
by Amazon

48842571R00129